Beyond th

Lisa Selvidge completed a BA in R
at the University of London, with Po
travelling around Asia and teaching English as a Foreign Language
for several years in Japan and Russia, she went on to take an MA
in Creative Writing (Prose Fiction) at the University of East Anglia
in the UK. She subsequently taught at the Norwich School of Art
& Design for five years and then at the University of East Anglia
where, in 2001, she became the Academic Director for Creative
Writing in the Centre for Continuing Education.

In 2004, she moved to Portugal where she now lives for most of
the year. She still teaches online prose fiction courses for the UEA,
Oxford and York, as well as doing workshops and writing retreats
in the Algarve. She is the author of *The Trials of Tricia Blake*
(fiction), *A Divine War* (fiction), *The Last Dance over the Berlin
Wall* (fiction) and *Writing Fiction Workbook* (non-fiction). She has
also edited a collection of writings from seventeen authors inspired
by the Algarve, entitled *Summer Times in the Algarve*.

For more information visit www.lisaselvidge.com

BEYOND THE SEA

Stories from the Algarve

Published by **Montanha Books**
Apt 8, Monchique 8550-909, Algarve, Portugal
Contact: info@montanhabooks.com

'The Big Doll' was first published in the anthology, *Summer Times in
the Algarve*, Montanha Books, 2008

Printed by lulu.com
www.lulu.com

Typeset in point 11.5 Times New Roman

ISBN: 978-0-9559856-2-1

Cover image and illustrations by Anja Paulsen
Contact: anja k paulsen@hotmail.com

Cover design by Verónica Castagna
Contact: veroenmallorca@hotmail.com

Beyond the Sea

1. Arrival

Now that the man in the aisle seat next to her had shut up, Zoe closed her eyes and tried to relax in the humming plane, but all she could see was the young kid pointing a gun at her. She'd only asked him to read a passage from *The Merchant of Venice*. After two long minutes, during which she saw her life splattered in red on the whiteboard behind her, she'd managed to persuade eleven-year-old Thomas to hand over the gun. Sign of the times, she'd been told later in the staff room. It was April 2007, her second term at an inner city comprehensive school in East London, and she was finding it tough. The head had suggested she take some leave so now she had just over two weeks, until May 4th, away from guns and twelve-hour days. Two weeks to relax with her old school friend, Maria, and think about her life and where it was going.

The 'Fasten Seat Belts' sign binged as the plane tilted out of the blue sky towards the sunlit city of Faro. The man next to her began to snore loudly, his large nostrils flaring as he inhaled. He had dark cropped hair, a fuzzy moustache, a goatee beard, and a very loud voice which oscillated between a public school and an American accent.

'Even asleep he doesn't shut up,' Maria whispered, pushing her glasses onto her nose. The large, round, black-rimmed glasses with thick lenses gave her an air of authority which the kids in the library where she worked seemed to respect. Zoe had thought about buying a pair, even though she didn't need them.

The man had talked non-stop since leaving Gatwick until five minutes ago. His name was Ed, and he was coming to the Algarve to buy it, apparently. He told her (in the American accent) that this was *THE* country to invest in. It had everything – white sandy beaches, a climate akin to California, a turquoise sea, golf courses, a passion for football (he was a Chelsea supporter and fully approved of Mourinho), an upmarket tourist industry, a moderate government – left-wing but in a Blairish right-wing kind of way –

7

marinas and, most importantly, still cheap real estate. This was THE place to be. This was the new California of Europe.

'Sounds great,' Zoe said, trying not to be put off the Algarve before she got there. 'How often do you come here?'

Turned out this was his first time, he'd just read the brochures. But, despite images of golf courses and property developers, Zoe felt her heart warm as the crew were told to take their seats for landing.

'Hey there, I must have taken a nap,' Ed said, shuffling himself. Zoe's seat shuddered. 'Are we nearly there, girls?'

Zoe felt Maria flinch as she leaned over her friend to look out the window; 'girls' were what they called eleven-year-olds. White houses and oblong blue strips bandaged the orange land, and shallow turquoise lakes and mud flats stretched to the azure coast.

'Yep, we're about to land on the beach,' Zoe said, as a long ribbon of white sand came into view.

'Perfect. London's a great city but the weather sucks. Let me see,' he said, leaning over her so that his pink ears were almost in her face, 'And it's only April. Sweet!'

As Zoe stepped off the plane and into the sun, her heartbeat jumped and pulse raced as if she had suddenly come to life. Strands of her dark blonde hair turned to gold and her skin tingled. She stopped and inhaled the warm sun-dried air. Even the airport diesel smelled exotic. A caterpillar bus came to pick them up and serpentined ten metres to the airport while everyone from the plane took off jackets, pulled up sleeves, wiped foreheads, rummaged around for sunglasses. Mobiles beeped as they picked up the Portuguese networks. The school bells were beginning to fade.

Zoe passed through Immigration with only a cursory glance at her passport – unlike Gatwick where she'd had to take off her trainers, her face wash and cream had been confiscated and her body patted by hands in latex gloves. The luggage bounced onto the carousel behind stacks of golf clubs and soon they were ready to head for the 'Nothing to Declare' opaque doors.

'See you later, girls,' Ed shouted to them as he passed with an enormous suitcase rolling dutifully behind him. 'Have fun!'

'You too!' Zoe said, following a group of golfers.

'Thank goodness, he's gone,' Maria said, firmly pushing her glasses onto her nose again, punctuating her sentence.

'Don't speak too soon,' Zoe said.

The airport smelled of pastries, coffee, cigarettes and almonds. Dark Portuguese men with puppy eyes hung around, smoking, some holding up signs for people. Then they heard Ed talking to his mobile while standing in a queue at the Hertz desk. 'PORTIMAYO? How do you pronounce that?' he shouted at the woman behind the desk. '*MAO*? Like Chairman Mao? Did you hear that, Collette? You're sending me to some goddamn communist port!'

'What a character,' Zoe said.

'Well, he should get on well here. They say the Portuguese listen to the one who speaks the loudest and for the longest,' Maria said. She had been coming here for several years and knew a little about the country and the language. 'Only with any luck no one will understand him. I heard what he said when you told him you were a teacher in East London.'

'About being on the frontline in the fight against terrorism?'

Maria nodded. 'He's the kind of person who gets us into wars in Iraq for no reason. But, anyway, frontline fighters need to get the bus into Faro and then the train to Lagos. This way.'

As Zoe followed Maria out through the tinted airport doors she felt like she'd been blasted onto another planet. The air was scented with rosemary, thyme, orange and citronella. She sniffed it all up, the cold grey air dipped in salt, vinegar and curry of East London now a distant memory. They stopped at the bus-stop.

'It's a bit of a trek, I'm afraid,' Maria said.

'That's okay, we have all day. In fact we have sixteen days. Fantastic!' Zoe said.

Maria's parents had bought a small apartment three years ago in a place called Luz, and came out regularly during the winter. Maria could stay whenever she wanted. She had immediately invited Zoe when she heard what had happened. They were to stay at Maria's parents' apartment for ten days. Then, as her parents were coming out for a few days, Maria had booked a one bedroom apartment further down the coast in a small fishing village called Salema for an extra seventy-five pounds each. Zoe was very grateful as there wasn't much of her wages left each month after she'd paid her rent, council tax, electricity, water bills, phone bills, travel card, and basic food rations. To say nothing of the twenty-two thousand quid university debt.

A suitcase thundered towards them.

'Hey girls. Wanna lift?' Ed called to them, dangling car keys between his thumb and forefinger.

Zoe stopped and looked at Maria uncertainly. She didn't really want to spend another hour next to him. But a lift would be nice.

'Where are you going?' Maria asked him.

'I'm going to Portimão,' Ed said.

'No, that's okay, we're going to Luz. It's much further,' Maria said.

'I have until three o'clock. I'm more than happy to give you a ride. Come on, we're in Portugal! The sun is shining, the sky is blue. Allow me to buy you lunch in Luz?'

Zoe blinked at Maria. Surely she wouldn't agree. He was the kind of person who got them into wars in Iraq.

'Okay,' said Maria. 'But we'll buy you lunch. Thank you.'

Zoe's newly beating heart plummeted a scale but not for long. They would be at the beach sooner.

'Come on, where's the car? Let's go Portugal!'

They found the car, a blue Megane. Ed threw the heavy suitcases into the boot and onto the backseat as if he were arranging paperback books.

'I'm sorry one of you will have to squash on in there,' he said.

'That's fine,' Maria said, jumping in the back, leaving Zoe no choice but to get in the front.

'Where do I go? Does anyone know?' he asked as he drove out of the car park.

'Yep,' Maria said. 'You need to follow the signs to the A22 to Portim...'

'Mao!' he said. 'The woman at the hire car desk told me.'

'Look at those little moon men on the roundabout,' Zoe called out, gazing at the stone sculptures, their heads tilted upwards, in the middle of the roundabout. She was already enchanted by this new planet.

'Sweet!' Ed said, glancing across to the roundabout. 'Hey, look, that looks like a cool show. *Vida!*'

Zoe looked at a billboard advertising several upside down half-naked women. Underneath it said, 'Casinos do Algarve'. She looked behind at Maria who rolled her eyes in horror.

They drove past thousands of lonely silver hire cars, gleaming in the sun. Nestlé and Coca-Cola flags rippled from poles.

'Take the next right,' Maria said authoritatively.

'Okay.' He turned off and onto another road.

'There's a "give way" sign at the end of this slip. You need to stop.'

'But it goes onto a dual carriageway!' Ed said, continuing.

Zoe put her hands on the dashboard as he braked. Hard.

'JESUS! Who the hell would make a junction like that? Sorry, girls.'

'I think these junctions were made in the old days when there were only a few donkeys and carts,' Maria said, diplomatically. 'The newer ones aren't like that.'

Ed drove slowly along the dual carriageway and Zoe gazed at an old watermill, abandoned in the red earth, and at colourful ruins dressed in graffiti. As they approached some traffic lights, she tried to read the signs outside the shops, garages and restaurants: *Frango piri-piri, Churrasqueira, Pneus, Super Bock, Delta Café*. On a bridge crossing the road was scribbled, *Fora Capitalistas!*

'What does "fora" mean?' Zoe asked.

No one knew.

On one side of the street a brand new Porsche and a Mercedes were elevated above the car showrooms while, on the other, gypsies drove a cart and horse with three other horses trotting behind. A woman with two children sat in the back, their heads wrapped in coloured scarves.

'Wow, real gypsies. You never see them any more in the UK,' Zoe said.

'Except begging on Oxford Street. And on the tube. And in most other parts of central London,' Ed said. 'Usually with a bundled up baby to make you feel bad if you don't give anything.'

'They're not usually Romanies,' Zoe said, wishing they were nearly there. He would be on about the Poles soon and then Maria would probably slit his throat.

'Whatever. They're gypsies. They all come to London because they know they can get a free lunch.'

'Well, I've never had one,' Zoe said, trying to change the subject.

Ed smiled. 'Of course not. You're English. But when you're back in London, I'll buy you lunch with great pleasure.'

Oh no, he was flirting with her.

'So, do you give them anything?' Maria called from the back.

'Like hell do I. You feed these people and then they turn round and kill you.'

'Oh, I think that's a bit of a generalisation, don't you?' Maria said.

Zoe let out a hollow laugh. She didn't want to encourage either of them. And she certainly didn't want to get onto how someone had tried to kill her. He would love that. As would the tabloids. *Young Pakistani boy pulls gun on English teacher when asked to read a passage from Shakespeare* – even though his name was Thomas and had never even seen Pakistan. *Terrorism in the classroom! Shakespeare under threat!* The politics of fear at work.

She had met his parents at a parents' evening. His mother, a large, pale but beautiful East Ender, dressed in a pink headscarf, was not very articulate and Zoe was afraid that Thomas would get a clout around the ear when his mum got home, but Zoe remembered his father as being eloquent. The father was of Pakistani parents, but born in Leyton, and was shocked that his son had got hold of a gun. Zoe reckoned the older kids were dealing in weapons and that's how he had got it. She knew Thomas to be a bit of a loner, like most only children. Fortunately, the school had managed to keep it away from the press. They'd all had to go to the police station but Zoe hadn't pressed charges. He was just a confused kid. And there was enough confusion in the world.

'I bet you don't find many immigrants here,' Ed said.

'Well, only a quarter of a million Brits,' Maria said.

'They don't count. They're not exactly living off the welfare state, are they?'

'No, but they're not exactly contributing much either,' Maria snapped.

'Like hell they are. They have property, they shop here, they go to restaurants. They are part of the tourist economy – which is the one and only industry of the Algarve. I mean, come on, how many factories do you see?'

Maria leaned forward, repositioned her glasses and poked her head between the seats. Zoe sighed and looked out the window towards a large, elegant football stadium. Carpets of yellow and green clover looked like they had been thrown down on each side of the road.

'There used to be. Sardine factories in Portimão and Tavira. It was a big industry. And cork, of course. But that's not the point. My parents, for example, pay twenty-six euros each in council tax. That's not exactly a significant contribution and that's all they pay.'

Ed shrugged. 'The English bring a lot of money into Portugal. And the Dutch, Germans, even the goddamn Russians…'

'You take the second right here onto the A22,' Maria said.

They passed a sign indicating no pedestrians and no carts.

'There's no cars!' Zoe said, amazed, as they zipped along the new, empty dual carriageway. Distant villas sat comfortably in the terracotta hills, surrounded by palm and pine trees.

'Isn't this fabulous? New roads, no cars, no immigrants…' Ed winked at Zoe.

'Ha, ha,' Maria said crossly, but Zoe could tell she wasn't really angry.

They passed an old white Renault 4 snaking along the slow lane. A man was drinking from a bottle, the other hand on the steering wheel, a cigarette lodged between his fingers.

'That reminds me of a joke I heard when I first came to Portugal,' Maria said. 'Do you want to hear it?'

'Fire away,' Ed said.

Maria leaned forward.

'Okay, so it is Zé's birthday and he's invited out to lunch by a group of friends. He puts on his best Sunday clothes and drives his Renault 4 down to the local café for a coffee and a couple of brandies. Well, it is his birthday so he has a couple of small beers with some of the locals. Then he drives to the restaurant and meets his friends and they have soup, olives, bread for starters, wild boar for the main course and six bottles of red wine. His friends give him a bottle of whiskey as a birthday present. They eat, drink and sing Happy Birthday to him. Then they order coffee and brandies. At last, Zé says goodbye to his friends and stumbles to his car with his bottle of whiskey, and gets in. "Just a sip," he thinks, and opens the bottle. He starts the car and drives merrily along singing loudly. Then the GNR – the Portuguese police – overtake him and park in front of him so he has to stop. He almost crashes into them. The policeman comes over.

"So Senhor Zé, how much have you had to drink?" the policeman asks him.

"Well, it's my birthday," he slurs, "so I started with a couple of brandies and then two small beers and then I met my friends and we had six bottles of wine, a brandy and then I had this bottle of whiskey." He holds it up to show them.

"Hm. Would you like to breathe into this?" The GNR holds a breathalyser in front of him.

"Why?" Zé asks in surprise. "Don't you believe me?'"

Ed and Zoe laughed and the immigration tension dispersed out the windows. Zoe was impressed: she could never remember jokes.

'There's a cement works,' Maria said as they passed an enormous quarry.

'Ha, yes, to build the houses for the tourists!' Ed laughed triumphantly.

Zoe closed the window and they all fell silent as the car sped through the Algarve. They passed signs to Lagoa and Silves, crossed the river Arade, on their left an elegant bridge held up by white rays. In the distance, high rises cubed the horizon.

'That's Portimão. We want Lagos Oeste/Vila do Bispo, Junction 1,' Maria said.

'Okay.'

'So how long will you be here for?' Zoe asked Ed.

'That depends on the scale of investment we decide on. I expect to be spending much of the next six months here but I will have to keep going back to London.'

'I don't think there is much left to develop,' Maria said. 'In the five years I've been coming, they haven't stopped building. The road from Luz to Burgau and almost all the way to Salema is being built. Quarter of a million pounds for a 2-bed townhouse.'

Zoe yawned. Immigrants, property prices, houses in the sun, threats of terrorism, global warming, global economy and carbon footprints seemed to be the verbal diet of the early twenty-first century.

'There's still cheap property out there,' Ed said. 'Look around. There's no one here.'

He was right. Zoe couldn't wait to get into the sea. To swim, lie on the beach, eat fish, drink wine, read books. She had brought *Atonement, House of Meetings* and some non-fiction, *The God Delusion*. Judging by the weight of Maria's suitcase, she had brought half the library with her. Maria had warned that it would be quiet at this time of year but, who knows, she may even meet a man. A gorgeous Portuguese boy with smooth golden skin, those milk chocolate eyes and curly black lashes. Preferably a Taurus as she'd recently read that as a Gemini, Taurus was her perfect partner – not that she really believed in such things but you never know. They would fall madly in love and live in a little house by the sea. She would get a job in a school teaching English. After work, they would watch the sun set over the beach together before grilling fish on a barbecue and sitting under the stars with a glass of cool white wine.

Zoe had almost forgotten what it was like to have a relationship. She had shared her university years with Marcus but, after graduating, he'd gone on to do a Teaching English as a Foreign Language certificate while she had opted for an exhausting Postgraduate Certificate in Education. His course had lasted six weeks and then he'd disappeared into the Golden Triangle in Thailand, while hers had grinded on for a year. He'd obviously met someone, or stoned himself into oblivion, as he hadn't been in touch for more than fifteen months. She'd been out with a few men but no one who'd turned her legs to jelly. The only person who'd managed that had been eleven-year-old Thomas.

'Junction 1 is the next one,' Maria said, as they sped past a small truck, its open back crammed with furniture. The wardrobe on top looked like it could slide off any minute. Zoe smiled. That would never be allowed in the UK. She waited for Ed to say something but all he said was:

'I'm already liking this country.'

As they turned off the motorway, Zoe opened the window again and let the warm blue air whistle into the car. Dotted into the hills were white villas surrounded by cypresses, umbrella pine trees and white and pink blossoming fruit trees. Palm trees with punk haircuts poked the blue sky, others looked like giant pineapples. The earth, where it wasn't covered in green leaves and yellow flowers, was red-brown like dried blood.

They turned right at the next roundabout towards Vila do Bispo.

'The other way is Lagos – there's lots of good bars and restaurants,' Maria said.

'Hey, maybe we can go there later,' Ed said.

'And the Cultural Centre and Library,' Maria added.

They passed an immaculate villa estate with green lawns and sprinklers and then turned left to Luz. The narrow road took them down towards the sea, which lay below them like a silk blanket hugging the armchair bay.

'Forty-five minutes. Not bad. Do you want to drop your things off and then we go for lunch?'

'Yes, that would be good,' Maria said.

The apartment was on the second floor in the middle of an estate of white apartments and small villas. It smelled of trapped sea air and darkness. Maria opened the shutters and windows so that light

15

beamed into the rooms while Ed insisted on bringing in their bags. Zoe smiled at him. She had never known a man to do that. It must be a generation difference; she reckoned Ed was about fifteen years older than her.

'Hey, this is sweet,' Ed said, striding through the lounge out onto the balcony. Zoe followed him. A square of sea shimmered between the white houses, bougainvillea and palm trees. It was more than sweet. It was beautiful. What a contrast to Leyton. To think both worlds existed at the same time.

'How much did your parents pay for this?' he asked Maria.

'A hundred thousand pounds three years ago. They knew the couple who were selling it. They used to stay here so I think it was a bit of a special price.'

'It's fantastic,' Zoe said. 'Imagine having somewhere like this you can come to whenever you want.'

'You will have one day,' Ed said.

Zoe thought that highly unlikely. And the odds were stacked against her teaching in an inner city school.

They walked to the beach. The golden sand stretched down to a turquoise sea surrounded by biscuit-layered yellow and orange cliffs that curved around the bay as if a giant had taken a big bite out of the land.

There was a square with several people sitting outside. They all looked English. There were signs for beans on toast, full English breakfast and poached egg on toast. A tall woman with blonde hair and blue eyes cleared a table. She came up to them.

'You sit here,' she said in a thick Slav accent.

Zoe looked at Maria and they almost laughed. She was either Polish or Ukrainian.

'No, we're good, thanks,' Ed said to her. 'That restaurant looks cool.' He pointed to the beach bar.

'What's wrong with this place,' Maria said. 'It's our treat remember.'

'No, girls, I insist. Come on, let's enjoy ourselves.'

Zoe would have been quite happy sitting on the pavement but they followed Ed to what looked like an expensive wooden beach restaurant.

'Look, there's a table for us,' Ed said, striding ahead. 'Waiter, we want that table.'

'Oh no,' Maria muttered.

Zoe laughed.

16

They sat down at the table Ed wanted on the terrace while a waiter with those milk chocolate eyes and short dark hair gave them menus. Maria was a vegetarian but she ate fish so they decided on prawns – *camarão*.

'What wine do you recommend?' Ed asked the waiter.

'A *vinho verde* is good for lunch and *camarão*.'

'*Vinho verde*. Then we will have this one here.' His finger hit the bottom of the list.

'But that's twenty-five euros,' Zoe hissed.

Ed shrugged. 'My treat. Would you like a bottle of white as well?'

'No thanks,' Maria said curtly. 'But can we have a bottle of water please?' she asked the waiter.

The waiter nodded and wrote everything down.

'They're all men who work here,' Zoe noted as the waiter disappeared. 'I wonder why.'

'Maybe because the men need to support the women and the families,' Ed said.

'Do you think it still works like that here?' Zoe asked.

'It still works like that in most places,' Ed said.

Zoe thought she detected just a trace of bitterness in his voice.

'No, it doesn't,' Maria said.

'At least they're Portuguese here.' Ed winked at Zoe.

Fortunately, the waiter appeared with a basket of bread, butter, sardine paste and olives. Then the wine appeared together with an ice bucket. The waiter poured it.

'Cheers girls! Here's to our time in Portugal!'

They all clinked glasses and tasted the soft, sparkling white wine and murmured their approval, even Maria. Zoe melted into the setting. It was paradise. Some local boys, their little bodies like roasted chestnuts, played in the waves. A small blonde-haired girl, intent on building a sand castle, patted the fine grains with a small spade while their parents sat under an umbrella playing with two younger children.

'What a perfect world for kids,' Zoe muttered.

'It's pretty perfect for adults,' Ed said.

'Kids are very much a part of Portuguese life,' Maria said. 'They are always included. Maybe that's why they always seem to be well-behaved. Not like in England.'

The turquoise sea gushed back and forth ironing out the churned-up golden sand. Mesmerised, Zoe wondered at different lives, and the geographical and social randomness into which everyone was born. How would she be different if she had been born into an Algarvian fishing family? Or if she were a daughter of a surgeon in Lisbon? Or a daughter of a politician in America? Or a daughter of a beggar in Romania? Or a daughter of a suicide bomber in Pakistan? It was all so random. And, then, family and society instil certain traditions and expectations, making it almost impossible for anyone to escape their upbringing or to change their destiny. But not entirely. Zoe's mother worked in the meat hall in Leicester market and her father was an occasional builder with long periods unemployed. Zoe had managed to become a teacher, a professional. She had managed to change her social destiny, and yet, somehow, looking around, she felt it wasn't enough. She wanted more. She carefully folded a napkin as she wondered if that was so wrong?

The *camarão* arrived and they all dived into them.

'Delicious,' Ed said, crunching through the heads as well.

'Um,' said Maria, for once in agreement with Ed.

'So what do you do in London?' Zoe asked.

'I'm a stockbroker. I gamble with other people's money. But as well as the usual oil, telecoms and dotcoms, we're looking at going into property development. Some of our customers want more security.'

'So it has nothing to do with banking laws having more privacy here?' Maria said knowledgeably.

Ed gulped some wine. 'That is also an encouraging factor.'

'What do you mean?' Zoe said.

'It means it's very easy to launder dirty money,' Maria said.

'What like? Mafia money?'

'Well, you know, businessmen, politicians,' Maria replied.

'You work for the mafia?' Zoe asked.

'I'm afraid all information about our clients is confidential,' Ed said, winking at her.

'Is that what you did in the States as well?'

'Something very similar, yes, in fact, we have a partner in New York.'

Zoe raised her glass and stared at the slowly rising bubbles. She had never lived anywhere but Leicester and London. She wasn't sure if she liked either of them.

'I'm going to come and live here,' Zoe said. She had no intention of saying it but as she did, it felt right.

'Go girl,' Ed said, clinking her glass.

'You're just being seduced by the sun, sea and shrimps,' Maria said. 'I know lots of friends of my parents who've moved out here and are really unhappy. They become alcoholics.'

'Another bottle,' Ed said to the passing waiter.

'That's because they're not doing anything,' Zoe said. 'I'm going to get a job. There must be some schools here.'

'Yes, there is an international school, I think,' Maria said. 'But, Zoe, think of all those public school brats. You'll soon be wanting the real world.'

'Why don't you think this is real?' Zoe said. 'It's real for the people who live here.'

'Yeah, but it's not how most people live. They're the elite.'

'What's wrong with living with the elite?' Ed said.

Maria gave him a scathing look, as if she couldn't even be bothered to answer such a stupid question.

Ed dipped a prawn into the garlic sauce. 'You know if you put crabs in a basket and one tries to crawl out, the other crabs will pull him back down again. Zoe is trying to crawl out of the basket.'

Zoe laughed. In a way it was true.

'Well, for me, it's more about uniting with the crabs in order to pull apart a fisherman's basket so that we can all get out,' Maria said.

She had a point, Zoe had to agree.

Ed laughed. 'Oh well, I'm glad to hear good old socialism's alive and kicking in Europe.'

'I would just like to live somewhere else for a while,' Zoe said, lighting a cigarette. Maria wafted the smoke away.

'You do it girl,' Ed said, pouring out more wine.

'I mean I struggle to teach in an East London school. I have no social life, I have no money. I live in a shithole, I have big debts. What have I got to lose?' Zoe inhaled deeply, no longer sure if it was the wine speaking or her.

Maria shrugged. 'Think of all the kids you are helping.'

But Zoe couldn't help thinking that it was she who needed help at this moment.

'Here's to crawling out of baskets!' Ed said.

'Here's to uniting crabs!' Maria said, smiling at Ed.

They toasted, laughing, and sat back replete, the prawns all eaten.

'How do you say "thank you"?' Zoe asked.

'"Obrigada" for a woman, "Obrigado" for a man,' Maria said.
'*Obrigada.*'

'There's a *Portugal News*,' Maria said, reaching over to the table next to her and picking up a newspaper. 'You might find a job in it.'

Zoe flicked through it, beginning at the back, and her eyes fell on an advert for English and Mathematic teachers wanted at an International School in Lagoa. She blinked twice and her pulse increased just a fraction. It was as if someone had put it there just for her. When Maria went to the toilet she quickly tore it out. Ed winked at her.

'I think it's time for you to climb out of the basket.'

'I think you might be right,' Zoe said. Here was the job, here was the place. All she needed now was the man and a house by the sea.

'Hey, would you like to go out later?' Ed asked. 'Here's my card. Call me.'

Fortunately, Maria came back.

2. On the beach

'The sea bass is *espectacular*,' Zé said, stabbing his pen on his order book to emphasise how spectacular it was. 'You want I show you?'

'No, that's all right,' the mother said hurriedly. 'I think I'll have the fillet. And you, Jack?'

'I'll have the squid,' Jack said. He was reddish, baldish, fattish. Like most foreign men.

'A good choice, sir. One fillet, one *lulas*. And the young ladies?'

Zé flashed a smile as he gave the young ladies, presumably their daughters, his full attention. One of them had dark hair, a pale complexion flushed by the day's sun, and a small nose on which perched a huge pair of glasses. Not bad, but too serious. The other one though. She looked up at him. *Espectacular*, Zé couldn't help thinking, stabbing his notepad again. Eyes the colour of the sea on a winter's afternoon and long glittering blonde hair like rays of sunshine. She must be about twenty. Tourists. Always the best. He reckoned it was the family's first visit as he'd never seen them in Salema before. He checked her fingers which gripped the menu. Ringless. She tapped them against the black cover – as if she knew.

'I think I'll have the spinach lasagne,' the dark one with glasses said.

'One spinach lasagne,' Zé said. 'And you?' he asked gently, looking into the beautiful one's eyes. He knew northern Europeans found his dark eyes in particular irresistible. He was tall as well; an advantage over most of the other guys in the village when it came to girls. He was miles ahead of all of them. Paulo liked to think he was close, but he wasn't. Zé had slipped up by being engaged to a local girl for two years, but she had smashed up his car and left him last summer. He had learned his lesson. He really missed his car. A black VW Golf. She had driven it down a goat's track by the cliffs, hitting every boulder she could find, like a madwoman, and reduced it to a hideous piece of wheel-less metal.

'I'll have the *robalo*,' the beautiful one said.

'One *robalo*,' he said. 'Your accent is very good.'

'*Obrigada*,' she said, smiling at him. He felt ice sliding down his back and gripped the aluminium table to steady himself. He looked out to the sea but even that seemed to quiver like fish scales. The tide was out, the golden beach bathed in sunset.

She zipped up a blue jacket.

'You are cold?' he asked. 'You want to sit inside?'

'No, I'm fine, thank you. It's too beautiful here to sit inside.'

'Ah yes.'

The father ordered a bottle of Periquita without hesitation. Perhaps they had been to the Algarve before.

'Is this your first time in Portugal?' he couldn't stop himself from asking.

'Ah no, we come all the time. But it's the first time for Zoe.' The man indicated the beautiful one.

'I see,' Zé said, confused. She couldn't be their daughter if it was her first time, although the English had strange family arrangements. 'And you like?' he asked Zoe. Zé and Zoe, he found himself thinking.

'I love it. I'm thinking of coming back to live,' Zoe said.

Zé hesitated. That would be more complicated. 'You would like it very much,' he said.

He went inside and shouted the order through to the kitchen and asked Paulo for the wine. It was only the end of April and they weren't expecting to be busy, fortunately, as Benfica was playing Setubal. A few locals sat at the bar watching the pre-game hype. He joined them and lit an SG cigarette. Of course Benfica would win but FC Porto was ahead of the League. By one point. Then Sporting. By another point. Then Benfica. If both Sporting and Porto lost, there was a chance. The sound was turned down as the owner said that not all tourists liked to watch football. He said they liked to listen to the sound of the sea. But then he was German.

'*Bonita*,' Paulo said, passing him the drinks tray, indicating with a nod the table on the terrace.

'Hm.' Zé frowned at him. Paulo had lived in England and spoke good English, but Zé reminded himself that he needn't worry as Paulo nearly always got drunk and fell over. Or got into fights. Foreign girls didn't like that. Neither did Portuguese girls, for that matter. Besides, Paulo looked old. A woman had guessed he was thirty-eight last night. Ten years out.

'Do you think they want to go to the party later?' Paulo said.

'I doubt it. They are with their parents, at least one of them is – I think.'

'Shame.'

Zé poured the bottle of wine into the father's glass for him to try. He swilled, snorted, sipped and then said it was fine. The dark one looked at Zé strangely, almost angrily, out of her magnified eyes, fingering her glass. He leaned over the beautiful one. She smelled of cherries. She couldn't possibly be related.

'Thank you,' Zoe said. She smiled at him.

He felt an urge to roll about on the floor with her but he put one hand behind his back and poured the wine for the others.

The beautiful one pulled out a packet of Benson & Hedges. 'I can smoke here, can't I?'

'Of course you can smoke wherever you want.' He whipped out a lighter and bent over her. Big eyes wafted the smoke away.

'In England soon we can't smoke in restaurants or bars at all.'

'In Portugal there would be Revolution,' Zé said.

'The EU regulations will come here, too, you know,' the father said.

'Well maybe to one table.'

They all laughed. Zé felt good. He liked it when people laughed. They raised their glasses and he melted away to smoke the rest of his burning cigarette at the bar. The game kicked off but they'd only made a few passes when the baskets of homemade bread, olives, butter, sheep's cheese and pickled carrots in garlic appeared on the bar. He swiftly carried the starters on his arm and in his hands, and stood just behind the beautiful one as he positioned them onto their table.

'Do you stay here?' he asked the father.

'Well, we're in Luz...'

'*Golo!*'

Zé whipped his head towards the television for a split second. *Ahhh!* Simão was clutching his head. He'd missed. The evening suddenly wasn't looking too hopeful. Benfica hadn't scored, the beautiful Zoe was staying in Luz, fifteen kilometres away, and he didn't have a car.

A party of ten came in and the Paraíso was unexpectedly busy for the time of year. They'd had to close for a couple of months in winter as Hans, the German owner, said they couldn't afford to stay open. The small, fishing village emptied out as if the tide had taken everyone away. Almost everywhere closed. Zé had thought about going away himself but he'd spent all his money. Actually, he'd gambled most of it, but it didn't matter. He wouldn't know where to go anyway. England was too cold and, judging from the people who arrived here, too stressful. Besides, soon you couldn't smoke. He didn't speak such good German or French, and he didn't know anyone there. Here, he had a home, a mother who worshipped him, an older brother, who was out of work – not only during the winter – and he still had enough to drink at the Social Club. It was fine. It was winter. And now, he was earning good money. He enjoyed his job, especially when it was busy, and his head not too heavy. He'd started when he was twenty and this was his fifth year working at one of the top beach restaurants in the Algarve. Respect and discretion were the key. 'The customer is always right,' Hans told them. 'Even when they're not. Answer their questions, laugh when they laugh and disappear when you are not needed. Always be discrete. Never make assumptions. Never ever be disrespectful. And never sleep with them.' They'd all smiled on hearing that.

Zé glided from table to table, taking orders, drinks and starters. He had only time to check the score and it was still 0-0. Only fifteen minutes left of the game. *Parvos* couldn't score. FC Porto had as good as won. So had Sporting. If Benfica lost this one, they had lost the League. Every so often he looked over at Zoe. She always seemed to be laughing or talking. Her hands danced above the table as she spoke. The father ordered another bottle of wine with their meal.

'How long you stay for?' he managed to ask as he cleared the plates away.

'We're off tomorrow,' the father said. 'The young ladies here are staying for a few more days.'

Zé smiled and nodded. A Portuguese father would never allow his daughter to stay alone, but that boded well for him. If only he had a car.

'We've already been here for ten days or so,' Zoe said.

'*Golo!*'

He didn't need to look behind him to know that Benfica had scored. He sighed in relief as they ordered coffee with milk, as most foreigners did – and a brandy for the father, as most men did.

Maria and her mother asked for the almond tart. Zoe didn't want anything.

He hurried to the bar to get their coffees and brandy. Miccoli had scored. Thank God.

Their bill came to eighty-seven euros and the father told him to keep the change from a hundred euros.

'Thank you very much, sir,' he said.

After work Zé was surprised to see Zoe standing at the Azar bar talking to an English guy, Pete. The dark one with glasses was sitting next to her, drinking an *imperial*. No sign of the parents. He went up and stood behind Zoe. She was almost as tall as he was, but not quite. Slim, sexy and the cutest ass. She turned round immediately, as if she'd known it was him. She touched his arm and he felt his toes fall off. He smiled at her and looked deep into her turquoise eyes and knew then he would owe Hans an apology.

'Hey,' she said. 'You've finished work already?'

'Yes, eleven.'

'Would you like a drink?'

'A small beer?'

'Sure. *Três cervejas por favor*,' she asked José, the barman.

'Where is the parents?' he asked.

'They have gone back to Luz. We are staying here.'

Zé couldn't help grinning. Benfica had won. The beautiful girl was in Salema on her own. Almost. He just needed to find someone with a car to get them to the party. Other than Paulo.

'Where did you learn to speak English?' Maria asked him.

'Here,' he said.

'You've never been to England? America? No?' Zoe asked him.

He shook his head. 'Everyone tells me not to go. They come here and tell me that I have luck to live here.'

'But don't you want to see for yourself?' Maria poked her glasses back onto her face and stared at him with her big eyes.

Zé shrugged and drank his beer. 'Not really. Maybe one day.' Besides, he never had enough money. Foreigners didn't understand that. He would have to work a week to earn what they had spent on their dinner.

Pete had a car and he might want to go. He asked him but Pete said he had to work the next day. Just as Zé was ordering more drinks, Paulo came in. Paulo immediately went up to the two girls and put his arms around them.

'Hey, girls, fancy coming to a party later?'

Zé wanted to punch him but then Zoe asked Paulo if Zé was going. Zé nodded and grinned at Paulo.

Cabrão, you've as good as emptied your balls, Paulo said to him and then, turned to the girls. 'Then we all go.'

'What kind of party?' Maria asked. She seemed more relaxed after a few beers. Zé handed her another one.

'It's like a rave out near Barão São João,' Paulo explained. 'There's some New York guy DJing. It's the first party of the season.'

'Sounds cool,' Zoe said. 'How do we get there?'

'In my car.'

'But you're drinking?'

Paulo shook his head. 'Only beer.'

The girls laughed when they saw Paulo's Renault 4. Admittedly, it was almost as dented as Zé's VW, but it had wheels. Maria nearly refused to get in, especially when she was told she would have to hold on to the door as it sometimes fell off.

'Are you sure this is legal?' Maria kept asking.

'Quite sure. But we go the back roads,' Paulo said, driving off.

'I think my grandmother had one of these back in the sixties or seventies,' Zoe said.

'Look at where the gear stick is!' Maria said.

'It's cute. I like it.'

'Apparently, it's against EEC regulations,' Paulo said. 'They don't make them any more.'

'Why?'

'Who knows? I even have lights. Okay, hold onto that door, we have to go on the 125 for a short way,' Paulo warned.

It was gone midnight: the roads were empty, but the GNR had a habit of setting up road blocks and stopping old cars. If you were young and blonde you might get away with it, but Paulo would be screwed. He didn't even have a licence. Fortunately, there was no one. They turned off the main road and back onto the country roads.

'Do you come here often?' Zoe said, leaning forward. Her warm breath tickled Zé's neck.

'No, this is a new party. Every year is different.'

They bounced through a gate and down a track. Incandescent ribbon decorated the hedge and music thumped through the ground. They reached dozens of cars tilted on the side of the ditch. Paulo swung the Renault towards the hedge and switched off the engine. The girls clapped.

As soon as they got out the car, Zé put his arm around Zoe and they huddled together. He couldn't wait to be naked with her. Paulo walked in front with Maria.

'You are very beautiful, you know. You have a boyfriend?' Zé asked Zoe.

'No,' she replied.

Zé thought he sensed some form of hesitation. 'You should have a boyfriend. Maybe two?'

'Yes, maybe I should.' She laughed. 'And you?'

'I have four.' He knew she wouldn't believe him.

'Boyfriends?' She smiled at him.

He laughed.

'Look at the stars,' she said. 'What sign are you? Horoscope?'

'Sign? Oh I am the bull.' He put his hands to his head and pretended to charge at her. She wriggled like a fish out of water. He threw her over his shoulder and swung her round, laughing all the time. He put her down and pulled her towards him, his lips poised to kiss her.

'Come on, you two, hurry up,' bossy Maria called back.

'I'm Gemini. We're perfect for each other,' Zoe said.

'Of course we are,' he said, conscious of his mouth half open as she pushed him away.

He took her hand and they caught up with the others. There was a dance area where the DJ was mixing sounds and several tents selling bottled beer and red wine only. Zé paid the cover charge of five euros each and Paulo got the beers. They danced for a while and then Zé bought more bottles of Super Bock. He wanted to be alone with Zoe so he took her by the hand and they headed away from the party, past people huddled on the ground, smoking joints and watching stars.

'It's beautiful,' she said.

He found a secluded place in between some bushes, took his jacket off and put it on the stony ground for her. He put his arm around her and she turned to face him. Her eyes shone an electric blue in the moonlight. *Espectacular.* She kissed him. Deeply, passionately, lovingly. He felt he was being swallowed whole. He closed his eyes.

'Zé! Time to go to work!' his mother shouted. 'It's almost four o'clock!'

His eyes pinged open and he was relieved to find he was in his bed. Then he checked his pulse and panicked when he couldn't feel anything other than his head throbbing. He groaned as the previous night slotted into place. Paulo had stayed up drinking with him until about ten o'clock in the morning since Maria had refused to let them sleep in their apartment. Zé got out of bed with a heavy head and cut knees. He showered, got dressed and stumbled down the hill to the *pastelaria*. He needed a coffee and *Macieira*. He checked his phone and found three messages from Zoe. Before he had time to read them he saw her sitting outside reading a book. She had a large, floppy straw hat. He remembered them making love under the big dark sky. She was gorgeous, but he was feeling sick. And he didn't want any of the guys to see him with her. Gossip spread through the village quicker than it took him to walk up the hill.

'Hey, Zé, I thought we were going to the beach this afternoon?' she said as he approached.

'*Boa tarde*, Zoe,' he said, kissing her on both cheeks. 'How are you?'

'I'm fine,' she said. 'A little hungover. It was a great night though. I really enjoyed it.'

'Me too.'

'Why didn't you meet me?'

'I was sleeping. Paulo and I drink too much and now I have to take a coffee before work. Excuse me. We meet later, okay?'

'Oh, okay.'

He went into the *pastelaria*. The guys greeted him. Some of the older fishermen, including his uncle Rui, who was not much older than Zé, and his little boy, Marinho, were eating a plate of *percebes*. Marinho reminded Zé of himself at that age. Zé, too, had wanted to be a fisherman like his father. Like everyone's father back then.

'You look like you've been at sea today, Zé,' Rui joked. 'Hope you got a good catch!'

'The best yet – and I didn't get cold and wet at sea.'

'You would be cold and wet as you'd fall in drunk!'

Zé laughed, got his coffee and brandy and sat down with some of the younger guys who were talking about yesterday's game. Rui must be mad to still go fishing. He knocked back the brandy. It was like sticking his head in a bucket of freezing seawater. His eyes widened, his face burned and he began to feel a pulse. He could just about face work now. Zoe wasn't sitting there outside when he left the *pastelaria*. The messages said: *Ola Zé, r we goin 2 beach later? ... Im in the pastelaria, meet me here? ... Zé, where r u?*

She was waiting for him outside the Paraíso when he finished work.

'Olá Zoe,' he said, kissing her. 'What a surprise.'

'Why? Were you expecting someone else?' she said. Her voice cut him.

'No, I never have expectations. I go with the waves.' Although his brother was expecting him to go to the Social Club.

She smiled. 'Shall we have a drink?'

'Is that an invite?' He winked at her and she laughed. He hadn't made good tips that night – he hadn't been in the mood to charm the customers. Not that there had been many. 'Where is Maria?'

'She's tired. She's staying in.'

They went to a bar and she bought him several beers until, at last, he felt normal.

'Can we go back to your apartment,' he said, touching her hair playfully.

'No, Maria's sleeping. What about your place?'

'We would wake my mother.'

'You live with your mother?' She sounded astonished.

'Of course. I'm not married.'

'I'm not married either but I don't live with my mother.'

'How old are you?'

'Twenty-four.'

She was older than he thought. 'Here, it is difficult. We don't earn so much.' He offered her a cigarette. She took one.

'It's not so easy in England either. More than half my wage goes on rent, council tax, water bills. I'm only left with about three hundred pounds a month.'

It was about what he earned, not including tips.

'Aren't you going to ask me what I do?'

'What do you do?'

'I teach.'

'A teacher? That's good.' It was terrible. He had failed nearly all his exams and left school as soon as possible.

'Not really. I teach at a school in East London. It's very bad. The kids are always fighting. One walked in with a gun a few weeks ago.'

She talked some more about her job. He didn't understand everything, but he did understand that she lived in a different world. She had been to university. He had only ever read one book, *The Alchemist* by Paulo Coelho, because his brother said he should, and that had taken him a year. Even then he wasn't sure he had understood everything.

'Let's go for a walk on the beach,' she said.

Zé complied, not that he wanted to. It was windy. Foreign women always wanted to walk on the beach – even in the rain. But images of Zoe standing in front of a blackboard in a short skirt were warming him up and he doubted any of the older guys would see them. They took a couple of beers and, as soon as they were under the cover of darkness, they began kissing. Zé felt himself falling again. This girl was special. He found a place to sit semi-sheltered by the rocks. The wind whipped sand around them. The lights of the fishing boats flickered red and white out at sea.

'Look at the stars,' she said.

'Um,' Zé said.

'There's something very special between us, isn't there?' she said, pushing him down.

Zé agreed as he kissed her neck, his hands exploring beneath her dress. Dresses were so much easier than jeans.

'You are fantastic,' Zé whispered as they made love. She gasped as he moved inside her.

'Would you like to come to England to visit me?' she said, as they huddled back together smoking a cigarette.

'Only if I can smoke,' he joked.

'You can smoke with me anytime,' she said. 'I'm only here for another couple of days.'

'But you are coming back?' he said.

'Would you like that?'

'Of course.'

'Will you email me in the meantime?'

'I don't have a computer.' Even if he had, he wouldn't know what to do with one.

'There are internet cafes.'

'But, you know, I don't have so much time.'

'Oh. When is your day off?'

30

'Tomorrow.'

'Excellent. We can do something. Maybe take the bus into Lagos?'

The bus to Lagos? He always played football on the beach on his day off. He walked her home and promised he would see her the next day. Then he hurried to meet his brother in the Social Club, but he'd gone.

The next day, Zé got up in time for lunch. They had *feijoada* and rice. His mother had made his favourite chocolate mousse for dessert.

'How was work last night, Zé?' his mother asked.

'Busy, *Mãe*. We didn't finish till late,' Zé said.

His brother laughed. He had seen him go onto the beach with Zoe.

'You can't talk,' his mother admonished his brother. 'You don't even have a job. Did you make good tips, *filho*?'

'Not bad. Do you need some money, *Mãe*?'

'No, *filho*, you save up for your car. And make sure you're back this evening as your aunt and uncle and your cousins are coming round.'

After a strong *bica* coffee, Zé and his brother went down to the beach together.

Zoe was at the *pastelaria* again. This time she was sitting with João, the local dope dealer and Sasha, the mad Russian prostitute – so the rumours went – and Günter, an older German guy and his howling dog, who camped in a ruin. João and Sasha were wearing matching straw hats and purple sunglasses. Zé waved to them all as her eyes followed him. His uncle Jorge, Nuno and Romeo and a couple of their dogs were playing near the water's edge. His brother went to get some beers while Nuno passed him the ball.

Zé danced the ball on his knees before pirouetting around it and kicking it backwards to Jorge, who headed it twice before arching it to Romeo. Zé loved this. The warm sand crushed by the weight of the sea beneath his feet, the camaraderie between the guys, the control he had of the ball as he made it twist and turn and roll down his body. He could do this all day. When he was hot, he dived into the freezing sea to cool down. Eventually, they fell onto the sand, played out. His brother suggested that they go to visit Pete's. He had a pool and had invited them round. Zé remembered he had promised to meet Zoe. His brother saw his hesitation.

'It will be fun, Zé. Let's go and have some drinks with the guys.'
'Okay.'

They spent the rest of the afternoon in Pete's villa on the hill drinking beer. He received a text from Zoe asking where he was. He replied that he was sorry but he'd had to go home.

Zé, his brother and Jorge were late for dinner and his mother scolded them but she didn't seem that bothered. Cousins Esmeralda and João were there, and also Aunt Paula, Uncle Rui and their kids, Inês and little Marinho. Their dining table was crammed. They crunched their way through *camarão,* fried prawns, and drank more beer. After dinner, he excused himself and went to watch TV. The last thing he remembered was little Marinho coming to see him with a book saying that he had to learn to read.

32

He had a few hours before work the next day so he went down to the beach and joined the guys. He had slept for about twelve hours and his head felt clearer than it had for days. Nuno bounced the ball on his thigh while his uncle Jorge was telling Paulo about how a little English girl had been kidnapped from Luz, warning him not to go there in his car as the place was swarming with GNR and reporters. Zé's phone beeped a message in his short's pocket. It was from Zoe, asking if he wanted a coffee. He texted her to say he was on the beach. Maybe they could meet up later?

He heard someone call his name and turned round as the ball flew over his head. Zoe stood there in a purple bikini, arms crossed over her stomach. Her long hair whipped her face in the breeze.

Nuno winked at him and ran after the ball.

'Hi Zoe. Sorry about yesterday. I was sleeping.' He flashed her a smile.

'Yeah? I waited at the *pastelaria* for you.'

'Sorry. I had to be with my family. Then I sleep like a stone.'

'Okay but can we talk? Now.'

Zé glanced back longingly at his little group. 'Sure,' he said. 'Let's sit down.'

They sat down on the sand.

'Do you like me?' she said.

'Of course,' he said, not liking the sound of this conversation. He hadn't even had a beer.

'It's just that you don't seem to want to see me,' she said. Her voice cracked slightly as she said this. 'Not even have a coffee with me?'

Zé gazed out to sea. A sailing ship skimmed across the white silky surface. 'Of course I want to see you,' he said.

'But you're always with other guys.'

'They're mates,' he said limply.

'So you'd rather be with them than me?'

Zé had a feeling what he was going to say was wrong. 'Sometimes.'

'I see.' She paused. 'I may have an opportunity to come to work here – at the International School. I contacted them and they seemed quite keen.'

'But that's good for you, isn't it?' He knew she wanted him to say more but he couldn't – even though the International School was a long way away.

'I don't know. I need to think about it.' She got up. 'You know, Zé, you can't go with the waves all your life. One day you'll wake up alone on the beach.'

Zé shrugged, kissed her on both cheeks and said he'd see her after work. Then he hurried back to join his mates. These things took time. But surely she understood that. He would talk to her later.

She wasn't waiting for him after work. He went to all the bars but he couldn't find her. He went to her apartment but it was dark. Maybe they were sleeping. He would find her the next day. He went to bed sober, thinking of her.

The next day he received a text. *Sorry I made such a mistake. I thought there was something special between us.* He was going to reply but he didn't have any credit left on his phone. He went up to her apartment but there was no sign of her or Maria. He searched for her on the beach but she wasn't there either. She must have gone. He shrugged and looked around. Long, tanned legs stretched down to the sea. There were plenty more girls. Someone headed a ball at him. He caught it, threw it back and walked towards the *pastelaria*.

3. The end of the road

Robert put his nail gun down and picked up the hammer and some two-inch nails. He would need to use these for the floor joists. He glanced up towards the open velux and caught a glimpse of an eagle flying across the blue sky above the mountainous eucalyptus forests. He blinked – sometimes when he was working he forgot where he was. Then he heard the vacuum cleaner rumble to life. Quite why Rebecca insisted on hoovering while he was working he would never understand. But they were nearly there. The doors and windows were in, the bathroom was almost done, the IKEA kitchen should be coming next week. And then they would only have the outside to do. No more than six months. Fuck it. That was enough for today. He'd had a few too many *medronhos* last night and needed to rest.

He climbed down the ladder and headed for the small humming fridge in what would be the kitchen. The vacuum cleaner must have heard him as it went quiet.

'Have you finished?' Rebecca called to him

'Just about,' Robert said, taking a beer, ignoring her scowl as she approached.

'It's only three o'clock, Rob,' she said.

He was amazed he'd lasted that long. He took several mouthfuls of beer before looking at her but she was making her way towards the ladder. The first beer of the day cooled his throat and stomach, and made him smile.

'I thought you were going to do the stairs today?' she called back. 'So that we could start sleeping up here.' She was climbing up the ladder to inspect the floor.

'Tomorrow,' Robert said, his smile fading. 'But the floor's done,' he added, knowing that she'd find something wrong.

'There looks like there's a few nails sticking up and it doesn't look like you've sanded it yet.'

'That'll only take a minute.'

'And how long will it take to do the stairs?'

'A couple of days.'

Rebecca sighed. 'I wish we'd rented for another month.'

Robert drank more beer, determined not to let her get to him. He was not going to get stressed – he'd had enough of that working as an in-house carpenter for a chain of shops around West London. They should have rented for a bit longer but after April the rent would have almost doubled. The house was taking longer than he'd thought. Especially as they'd had the roof, the plumbing and electrics done, as well as the inside and outside walls rendered, before they'd moved lock, stock and bulging barrel to Portugal. But so what? They had a roof over their heads. It would be finished when it was finished – hopefully before the money ran out. Anyway, it was fun, building their own house.

Rebecca came back and looked at all the sacks of grout and cement which were piled up in what would be the lounge.

'Well, maybe we could put all this in the kitchen?'

'Why?' Robert asked. 'I'm gonna be needing it soon.'

'So we don't have to spend another night staring at it.'

'Ah Beks, you're supposed to sleep at night, not stare at bags of cement.'

They were sleeping temporarily in the lounge on a mattress on the floor.

'I just want one room away from the dust,' Rebecca said and burst into tears.

Robert put his beer down and went over to hug her. She fell sobbing into his sawdust covered arms. She smelled of white spirits.

'I can't go anywhere without seeing cement, sand, broken glass, rubble and more rubble and mess.'

'That's because it's a building site, Beks,' Robert said. 'You knew that.'

'I didn't know it would be like this and you said the house would be ready by March. We're already into May and we don't even have a room to sleep in.'

'Fuck, Rebecca, I'm doing my best.' He let go of her and drank the rest of the beer.

'And why do you keep drinking?'

'It's only a little bottle of beer, Rebecca. It's normal. Haven't you noticed that everyone around here drinks beer all day? I'm thirsty for fuck's sake.' He went to the fridge to get another, aware that he was getting angry.

36

'Robert, you're drinking every day – and not just beer. And we need to get this house done. You're not doing hardly anything. I've painted every wall, sanded, cleaned – while you're fucking drinking.'

'Don't start, Beks.'

'I'm not starting. I just want to move the bed upstairs tonight so can we get the floor ready?'

'It's not worth it. It still needs sanding. Then it will need oiling or varnishing, or whatever you want to do with it.'

'Well, sand it then. You said it wouldn't take a minute. Then I can at least treat it.'

Robert looked at her. Her lips had tightened and her normally light blue eyes had turned grey as if set in stone. She looked like her mother.

'No, fuck it, Rebecca – I've had enough for today.' Robert picked up his van keys and headed towards the door, the French doors he had made himself. He was not going to be made to do things when he didn't feel like it.

'Where are you going now?' Rebecca screeched after him. 'Fucking running away again!'

He didn't reply but kept on going, past the cement covered trowels and piles of bricks to the rubble area where his red van and the Discovery were parked. He wasn't running away: he just didn't want a scene. He would go for a drive and keep calm. He heard his new French doors slam and muffled screams as if someone was trying to gag her. He wished.

As he opened the van door, he saw their neighbour, Dona Maria, an old lady of about eighty, digging away with an *enxada* a few metres away. She was only about four foot high but as strong as an ox. She waved to him and called, '*Olá*'.

'*Olá*,' Robert called back.

Rebecca didn't like the fact that Dona Maria crossed their land to get to the road, but then Rebecca didn't like anything.

He started the van and drove off. Rebecca hadn't followed him. She wouldn't make a scene while the old woman was there so he'd been saved.

He would go and see some neighbours who were also renovating. There were seven of them, all from Leeds, including two women and two kids, but they didn't seem bothered about bags of cement. Then he changed his mind. He wasn't really in the mood to talk to people. He decided to head down towards Portimão. He could pick up some more paper for his belt sander.

His mobile played. He glanced down at it and breathed deeply. It was Rebecca. He wasn't going to answer it. They'd only end up arguing.

He drove along the eucalyptus lined road, glancing occasionally at the hills folding down to the west coast. Why was it nothing he did was right? She was constantly criticising and bickering. Anyone would think they'd moved to some bloody housing estate, not a beautiful mountain in the Algarve. They'd been together for eight years. He'd thought they would be together forever but the thought of being with her for another eight days, let alone eight years, made him worry. He'd thought she'd be happy here, he'd thought they'd both be happy here but he had to face it – it wasn't working out. The truth hit him hard as he braked around a corner. *It wasn't working out.*

He turned onto the main east-west road and saw the sea sitting there, calmly, immutably, on the south coast. Perhaps he would rent somewhere – then she could finish the fucking house. Perhaps he should just draw out the rest of their money and leave her to it? Then again, perhaps he should just have a drink and relax.

He began the descent down the mountain, past the black stumps of eucalyptus – victims of the 2004 fires. The bright orange earth and green hillsides had been turned to black and white and was only just beginning to show signs of colour again. Down and down the van wound. He could smell the brakes burning. The LDV convoy had seen better days.

He decided not to call in at Maxmat – no point. Instead, he went straight to Praia da Rocha and parked near the coast. He dusted his trousers down, changed his T-shirt, put on a smart, black jacket he had in the van, and walked along the intricate paved stones of the coastal path that led to the bars and restaurants and sat down at a little bar that sold beer for one euro. His litre of beer arrived with a grunt.

The people at the next table were large, pink and had northern English accents. They began to work out how much the food cost in pounds. Robert downed the beer, left a euro on the table and went to the toilets where he had a quick wash and combed his hair with his fingers. Fortunately, he'd had a shave that morning. He was feeling hungry so he decided he would go to the fish and chip restaurant nearby. He would never normally – both he and Rebecca stayed well away from the tourist and ex-pat haunts but, at that very second, he just fancied some fish and chips. There was only one other person on the restaurant's terrace. Robert ordered cod and chips and a large beer.

'You on holiday?' the large middle-aged woman with an apron, presumably the owner, asked him as she brought his beer.

'No,' Robert said. 'I live here – well, up the mountains.'

'Oh really? How do you find it up there? Does anyone speak English?'

'Well, there are a few English, Dutch, Germans renovating houses. But not many locals speak English.'

'Well, that's good then, isn't it? I mean you get to speak the lingo.'

Robert nodded non-committedly. Rebecca was learning fast but he wasn't doing so well.

'I keep trying but it's no good here. All our customers are English.'

'How long have you been here?' he asked.

'A year but we've only opened in March. It's all been much harder than we thought.'

Robert hummed sympathetically and the woman drifted off to the other table.

'Another beer please, Ann,' the other customer called.

The salt and vinegar reminded him of rain-sodden West London. Not that he missed it. Only the happier times he had with Beks. Then again, they'd hardly seen that much of each other during the week – they'd both been working. And they both worked Saturdays so they only had Sundays and holidays together. Since moving to Portugal six months ago they'd been with each other every day and night.

He ate the fish and chips, said goodbye and good luck to Ann and headed further into Praia da Rocha. It was still early in the season, and early in the evening, so there weren't many tourists around. The sports bars were blasting out various results and commentaries. Then he saw a sign outside: Chelsea versus Manchester United. Brilliant! The game had already started but there was still more than half of it to go. Rebecca didn't like football so he hardly ever got to see a game. He went inside. It was dark and the large HD flat screen beamed giant faces. The score was 0:0.

He ordered a beer and sat on a stool. A guy with dark short hair and a goatee beard sat next to him calling out to the television. Rob thought he was American but, loudly and clearly, a Chelsea fan. As Robert settled into the game, sipping his beer, he felt happiness slide up from his fingers and all the way down to his toes. This was the life. The man next to him turned and held out his hand.

'Ed,' he said simply.

'Rob,' he replied. They shook hands and together groaned when Drogba's shot hit the post.

Ed ordered a round of tequilas for the dozen or so people in the bar – nearly all male Chelsea supporters, except for two young girls of about twenty, who, judging by their giggles behind hands, appeared to be Man U supporters because of Ronaldo. Robert knew he shouldn't drink the tequila if he was going to drive home but, fuck it, maybe he wouldn't go back.

Ryan Giggs hit the top of the goal post.

'Hell, Chelsea, are you having a siesta?' Ed shouted at the television. 'Wake up!'

'Don't worry, Manchester are dreaming if they think they can win this game,' Rob found himself saying. 'Come on Blues!'

The game groaned on with neither side scoring but with plenty of fouls – Makalele, Ferreira, Ashley Cole.

'It's more like rugby,' Ed said, in a surprising public school voice.

'Are you English?' Rob asked.

'Of course, I'm English. What did you think?'

'You have an American accent.'

'Ah yes, I'm an Englishman with an American accent. I lived in the States for about fifteen years before my wife... Oh you asshole!'

Makelele was off-side.

'What did your wife do?'

'She had an affair, threw me out, changed the locks and stole most of my money. Go Chelsea!'

'Oh,' Rob said. At least, Beks wouldn't do that. Would she?

The game went into extra time and more beers until, finally, Drogba scored and the whistle blew. Rob and Ed jumped off the bar stools with their arms waving in the air. The other guys started chanting and beer slopped from glasses launched upward and outward, and scarves rainbowed over heads. Mourinho was thumping the air while Ronaldo had his head between his knees, clearly on the wrong side. The girls looked as if they would cry.

'Probably not a game to remember,' Ed said. 'But we won. We are the champions!'

'Yeah,' said Rob. 'We are the champions!' As he said that, he felt a sense of belonging that he hadn't felt for a long time.

'Yeah, Blues! Hey, you wanna come for a drink to celebrate? I know a good bar down at the marina.'

'Sure,' Rob said.

They left the sport's bar and headed further down the street. There were a few more tourists about now as well as noisy Chelsea fans and subdued Man United ones. Young girls in stiletto sandals and short skirts hung onto each other as they clattered past couples clad in cardies and pink and blue Crocs.

'How the hell anyone got the world wearing a plastic fence around their feet should be awarded a diploma for brainwashing. Aren't they just the most ugliest thing in the world.'

Robert agreed, glad that he hadn't worn his.

'Where you staying?' Ed asked.

'I live in the mountains.'

'No kidding? The upper Algarve?'

'Is that what you call it?' Rob said, laughing. 'Not the bedpan Algarve?'

'The what!'

'They say that the cloud on top of the mountains is God's bedpan.'

'Hey, that's not the real estate's line. Does it really rain a lot up there?'

'Yes.'

'Hm. But not as much as England right?'

'Possibly more. When it rains it's torrential. Why? You thinking of moving up there?'

'Not exactly but we're thinking of investing – buying up properties and renovating. I've been looking at quite a few up there that I think would be good investments for clients. The coast is fairly crowded – and overpriced. Are you renovating?'

'Well I was but I'm thinking of moving out,' Robert said. 'I'm having problems with my girlfriend. Think we may have reached the end of the road.'

'Then what you need is a good night out, man. Come on, we'll go to the marina later but first let's go to the casino.'

Before Robert knew what he was doing, he was following Ed into the dark glass doors.

'We'll get a beer and go win some money! You with me?'

Robert's hesitation lasted less than a second. Why the hell not? He was having fun. He never gambled normally. He could afford a twenty euro flutter. Ed changed a couple of hundred and then they headed to some slot machines and started pumping in the money.

To Robert's amazement, the right colour cars kept lining up and the money poured out. With the kerchink of the machines he ignored his mobile phone ringing. Yes! There was another line! For once it was money that rained torrentially.

'Hey, it's your lucky night! Come on, let's cash in and go see the show.'

'What show?' Robert asked.

'What show! Come on, man, you haven't lived. Have you not heard of the new show, *Vida*! These girls are hot. I met them the other night in the bar in the marina and they told me about it.'

Rebecca would kill him. Robert felt as if he'd been wired up and switched on: every light was burning. He switched off his mobile phone, ignoring the three missed calls, and went to cash in almost three hundred euros.

Robert bought the tickets and they were shown to a table in a dark room in front of stage. There weren't many people and all men apart from two couples. Ed ordered two *caipirinhas* from a waiter in a black tuxedo. Robert wasn't sure if that was a good idea after beer and tequila, but changed his mind when he sucked through the straw burrowed into the ice and lime. It was cold, sweet and bitter. And very strong. Perfect.

Robert's eyes fell open as the electronic music began and four young women hung upside down from the ceiling, their bodies erotically wrapped around ropes. They spun round and round, their glittering legs caressing the darkness, faster and faster until they were flying above them. One by one they landed on the stage and crouched, curled up, then slowly uncurled and grew and grew. This was more art than showgirl stuff, Robert couldn't help thinking. Beks would like this. Then eight tall dancing girls came on stage dressed as school girls in short skirts and suspender belts, stiletto shoes, glittering eyes and red lips. Robert changed his mind. At the back of the stage appeared two male dancers dressed as school boys. Robert sucked up some more *caipirinha*. One of the girls winked at Ed.

Ed had it sussed, Robert had to admit, as he watched the showgirls – their bodies supple, strong, muscular, sexy as they danced around chairs and each other. There were more dancers in the air – as the same four girls swung on hoops and one girl without breasts split open her legs so far they closed again over her head. Robert didn't know that the female body could do that. The dancing girls, now dressed up in feather boas and high boots, were a relief to watch after the contortionist. There was a wavering line between erotic and grotesque, Robert couldn't help thinking.

Then two chunky men, hairless and oiled, dressed in leopard skin shorts, posed in front of the stage. One of them slowly lifted the other as if he were a majorette's baton. Ed caught Robert's gaze and then rolled his eyes upwards as if hoping for a girl to fall from the ceiling into his lap. Or, maybe, he was trying to say, big deal, he could do that. Robert wasn't sure but he thought they were both glad when the girls came back, the disco ball started spinning and the girls danced with each other.

He had no idea what the story was supposed to be, especially when the girls ripped off their tops and he found himself staring at sixteen large breasts. Ed almost choked on his *caipirinha*. Robert blinked.

'Wow,' said Ed, after the girls had gone, the stage returned to darkness and he had stopped coughing. 'That was almost as good as Chelsea winning. I think I'm in lust,' Ed said, taking the bill from the waiter. 'Are you coming to this bar? I need to eat, I mean meet, this beautiful showgirl even though I have a goddamn terrible feeling she's taken.'

Robert knew that he should go home now. He'd had enough to drink, he'd had a great evening, it was time to go home. He knew from previous drinking bouts that he should quit before it was too late. He gave fifty euros to Ed to cover the drinks and a tip. The waiter nodded at him.

'Of course I'm coming,' Robert said. 'Are you going to wait for her here?'

'No, they'll be ages. You know what girls are like. We'll meet them at the bar.'

Robert didn't know what girls were like – Rebecca was always waiting for him – but he could guess. They would need to change out of their glittering knickers, shower, take their stage make-up off and then dress to go out.

The bar at the marina was dotted with glamorous people cradling *caipirinhas*. A covered chill out area offered cane sofas and low lighting. Inside, a DJ mixed house music and several people danced under mirrored balls.

'Whe-hey! This is swe-et!' Ed ordered more *caipirinhas* and they stood by the bar watching the action. 'Rock Portimão!'

The music pulsed through Robert's veins and he found himself moving to the decibels. Ed also put his drink down and started waving his hands in the air.

They danced and drank determinedly. At one point, Ed asked him about Rebecca.

'So what's the problem with you guys?'

Suddenly Robert wasn't so sure. He muttered something about her constantly criticising him. He was going to add that she was controlling, always moaning about his drinking, but he stopped himself. He didn't want to talk about it now.

Five of the showgirls arrived with a couple of Portuguese guys. Rob recognised one of them as the waiter who'd served them. The girls looked like giant pieces of candy floss and Robert found himself drooling over all of them. Ed immediately ordered more *caipirinhas*. Charlotte, who had dark hair with blond highlights pulled up into a pony-tail and still glittering blue eyes, sat on a bar stool, sighed and rummaged around her bag.

'So what did you think of the show?' she asked.

'I thought it was awesome,' Ed said. 'And you were the best.'

She smiled and held up her left hand. It had a wedding ring on it. Robert couldn't believe she was married. She only looked about twenty.

'Ah shucks,' Ed said. 'Life is just not fair.'

They laughed.

'But you're a dancer,' Robert blurted out. At least he hadn't said 'showgirl' which is what he meant.

'So?' Charlotte said, knifing him with those ice-blue eyes.

'So... you're too young to marry.'

She laughed. 'Where are you from?' She turned her back on him, towards Ed. 'So how many times have you been married?'

'Only once,' Ed said. 'Now very single.'

Robert turned away, deleting the snub, and found himself drawn to a blond one with skin as smooth as sandal wood. She was wearing a red, tight dress with a low top and a little black jacket which she soon took off. In her red high sandals she was almost taller than Robert – and he was 5ft 10.

'Did you enjoy the show?' she asked in a deep, husky voice.

Robert nodded, not trusting himself to speak. He thought himself good-looking, particularly with his sun-kissed hair and tan, but he'd had a few to drink and he sometimes said stupid things. Instead, they danced together, Robert constantly aware of those breasts next to him.

'Careful Vicky, he's going through a divorce!' Ed called.

'You're a one to talk,' she called back, before turning to him.

'What happened? End of the road?' Vicky asked.

'Yes!' Robert said. How did she know? Is that what happened to everyone?

'So is she here in Portimão?' she asked.

'No,' Robert replied. He put his arms around her and pulled her towards him.

'That's all right then.'

Robert laughed. That was all right then. Beks would never know. Ed bought more *caipirinhas*, and handed them to Robert and Vicky. Vicky gave him hers to drink as the two male dancers came over and she started dancing with them. Robert drank both. Then decided that Vicky was getting too intimate with one of the dancers who had an arm linked tightly around her and had sinuously moving hips.

'What do they think they're doing?' he growled, moving towards them.

'Hey, Rob, calm down, man.'

An arm grabbed him, and steered him away. It was Ed.

'Ah, don't worry about me,' Rob said, knocking back another *caipirinha*. 'Isn't she gorgeous?' he said, eyes rolling around Vicky dancing. 'And she isn't married.' He burst out laughing.

'Be careful not to upset her. She's got a lot of friends.'

'How could I upset her? Girls just can't resist me.' Rob laughed. He had never had problems getting a girlfriend – not that he'd needed to in the last eight years. But now was different. He was single. He knocked back another *caipirinha*, clapped his hands above his head and went towards Vicky, pushing the other two dancers out of the way as he approached. Vicky turned her head and frowned at him, then turned away to where one of the other dancers was – a small, skinny man, who wavered like an entranced cobra. Vicky imitated his movements. Rob, not to be outdone, did the same. He thought he saw people laughing and he wondered why as he was moving real good. He could feel the music rippling through him. He raised his hands dancing to some invisible flute before coiling back into his snake basket.

Robert became aware of a pounding light trying to get into his head. His mouth was full of grit and his body felt as if it had been trampled on by a herd of elephants. What the fuck had happened? Was he being held hostage in Iraq? He groaned, wiped his mouth and opened his eyes to be greeted by the sea rushing towards him about five metres away. Shit. He rubbed his throbbing eyes, sat up and, once his eyes were clear of sand, looked around. He was on Praia da Rocha, it was early morning, a few people were walking their dogs but the sunbeds were not out yet. His head felt as if it were full of cement and he was cold. What the hell had happened?

He flicked through his memory and began to feel sick as he couldn't remember a thing beyond being in that club in the marina with Ed and the showgirls. He looked behind him at the pukey coloured cliffs and the tower blocks that prodded the blue sky but they wouldn't tell him anything other than the fact that he was halfway between the marina and where he had left his van. He must have tried to get back, fallen over and crashed out. He was cold because he didn't have his jacket, which he must have left in the club. He slapped his jeans around his thigh pockets. He still had his mobile phone and, amazingly, his wallet. He opened it – only ten euros. Strange. He clearly remembered winning three hundred euros – surely he hadn't spent it all? His mobile phone was switched off. He left it like that. He wasn't ready to face reality just yet. He needed to think. He remembered dancing with Vicky, drinking more *caipirinhas*, did they say they were going to another club? Had he tried to follow them? Had they jumped in a taxi and left him swaying at the side of the road? He had visions of being on a street trying to get a taxi. But he had no idea how he'd ended up on the beach.

Robert hugged his knees, his head drooped onto his chest. How quickly life can change. This time yesterday he'd woken up feeling a little heavy but with the day ahead of him to do the floor. Beks would moan at him but he would have a few beers and everything would be all right. This morning he was on the beach feeling as if he was the one who'd been sanded. He hardly dared think what he would tell Beks. But what the hell? She'd had enough of him anyway. He would tell her the truth. Then, if necessary, he would

46

go for a swim and not come back. He switched on his mobile phone. It was 8.10 am and there were three messages and five missed calls – all from her. He called. He braced himself for the tsunami.

'Rob? Is that you? Are you okay?'

'I'm okay, Beks. I'm sorry.'

A moment's silence followed.

'You're okay? Where the hell have you been? I was worried. Where are you?'

Rob was surprised by her calm voice. He'd expected her to rip him to shreds.

'I'm in Portimão. I met this guy, Ed, and we went out drinking. I stayed at his place as I couldn't drive.' She needn't know the whole truth.

'But why did you have your mobile switched off? I was worried.'

Beks wasn't cross with him – that was a miracle. 'I'm sorry, Beks. I switched it off because I was angry and then I forgot about it. Listen, we'll talk when I get back, okay? Do you need anything from Portimão?'

'Some bread and milk.'

'Okay, I'll get some.'

'And Rob?'

'Yes.'

'I love you, you know.'

Rob blinked. His eyes felt gritty again.

'I love you, too,' he said. He knew as he said it that he loved her more than anything in the world. Hell, what had he been playing at last night.

'Hey and guess what?'

'What?' he said, his stomach lurching down a roller coaster.

'I did the floor! And I slept upstairs! It's beautiful watching the stars out of the velux.'

'How could you have done the floor?' he asked.

'I sanded it with the sander, cleaned it up and oiled it.'

'Wow,' he said limply. Suddenly, he wanted to be in their home, curled up on their mattress beneath the stars. He wanted to put his arms around her and stroke her blonde hair and kiss her long, dark eyelashes.

'Hurry home. See you soon.'

'See you,' he said.

He switched off the phone and folded it shut. He wished he could fold himself shut. He had been an asshole. That was it. No more booze. Waking up with a mouthful of sand, shivering on a beach, not remembering what had happened was not fun. This was not what he wanted in life. He stood up, feeling dizzy, and brushed off the sand from his T-shirt and jeans. There was no point in going back for his jacket. He had been lucky to only lose that and the money. Very lucky. He needed some coffee and some breakfast before driving. He would still be way over the limit if he were stopped. Not that that was likely in the morning.

He staggered up the beach, the sand tugging him like glue, to one of the rickety wooden staircases that clung to the cliffs. He held onto the handrail and pulled himself up, each step heavier than the last. He stopped as he retched some *caipirinha* onto the succulent bright pink spiky flowers that grew in the crevices. The steps were now cut into the cliffs and he slowly meandered his way up.

The fish and chip restaurant wasn't yet open so he went to the one euro beer place and ordered beans on toast, a coffee and an orange juice.

'A beautiful morning,' the waiter said to him.

'Yes,' said Rob.

'Rain tomorrow.'

'Really?' He needed to put an extra coat on the doors and windows and paint the concrete on the roof.

The waiter nodded authoritatively and went off to get his order. Another English couple, much older than him, arrived and ordered coffee and brandy. For a moment, Rob was tempted – a brandy would make him feel so much better – but he drank his orange juice, ate his beans on toast and inhaled his coffee. He then walked across to the Alisuper and bought some bread rolls and milk. As he walked out of the shop he felt faint again and found himself almost running towards a public toilet where, once inside a cubicle, he threw up his breakfast, barely digested. The reek of *cachaça* made him retch more but there was nothing left. He stood over the toilet feeling weaker than he'd ever felt. Perhaps he should ask Beks to come and get him? But that would mean telling her how much he had really drunk. No, he would be fine. She was giving him a second chance and he wasn't going to blow it. He splashed water onto his face and tried to wash his armpits. His blue eyes were red, his blond hair was dirty and now he needed a shave. He stared at the rough man in the mirror who looked closer to fifty than thirty.

48

He swilled his mouth out, stuck his head under the tap and then under the dryer.

By the time he left the toilet he was feeling a little more human. He retraced his footsteps from yesterday, along the cobbled coastal path. Fishing boats and yachts glided through the water, the sun now warming up. The van was just where he left it. It rumbled to life and he drove out of the car park feeling a whole lot better than he had done an hour ago. It was a beautiful day, he was alive and loved – despite being a tosser.

He drove past Lidl and the shopping centre. He half thought about calling into Maxmat and getting some sandpaper but he wanted to get home. Past LeClerc, another supermarket, and some gypsies in a horse and cart with four other horses trit-trotting, two either side. He turned onto the Alvor turning and approached the roundabout and his heart stopped beating. There was a road blockage by the police, the GNR – nearly every vehicle was being stopped. The police were flashing posters at the drivers.

Rob tried to breathe in and out slowly. Please, not now. Not when he'd just decided to turn his life round. He would be at least two times over the limit – if not more. Mike had been held in a police cell for the weekend for drink-driving. But maybe he would get lucky. He had heard that sometimes the police wouldn't pull over foreign registrations and hire cars as the paperwork was too much bother. The two cars in front of him were let by. He put his foot down to follow them, but one of the bastards waved a baton at him. Shit, shit, shit. He pulled over, wound down his window and looked at the police officer who was at least five years younger than him.

'*Bom dia. Fala Português?*'

Rob shook his head. 'English?'

'Identification and driving licence.'

Keep calm, Rob told himself, he had those. He found his driving licence in his wallet but then remembered that his passport had been in his jacket.

'I have lost my passport,' he said.

The police officer was examining his driving licence as if it were contagious. Eventually, after he had turned it over several times, he began to write notes. This took about fifteen minutes. Rob tried to remember how long it took for each alcoholic unit to clear from the body. He reckoned it was about two hours so he was about quarter of a *caipirinha* clear when the officer turned to him again. He did a rough calculation and reckoned that probably meant he was still left with about six and a quarter.

'Passport?'

'I lost it. Last night. I need to contact the British Embassy.'

'Get out of the vehicle please,' the police officer said.

'Why? What is wrong?' Rob replied, trying not to breathe over the uniform.

'We need to search the van. It is open?'

Rob switched off the engine, snatched out the keys and opened the door. He landed on jelly legs and wobbled to the back of the van. His hands shook as he put in the key and opened it. Two policemen and an Alsatian dog swarmed round. They jumped in.

'What is this about?' Rob asked. 'What are you looking for?'

At least he had no drugs in the back. In fact, there was little at all apart from a couple of bags of cement and half a dozen boxes which they still hadn't unpacked but which were now being

50

opened by the police and sniffed by the dogs. Rob dreaded to think what was in them. Beks had been in charge of all the packing.

'Where you come from?'

'England.'

'I know that. Where you stay? Last night.'

'Oh,' Rob laughed. 'I see. Portimão.'

'Portimão? You are there all night?'

'Yes.'

'Where you sleep?'

'With a friend in Praia da Rocha.'

'You live there?'

'No, I live near Monchique.'

'Have you seen this little girl anywhere?' The policeman showed him a photograph of a little girl with blond hair, dark eyes, a haunted expression.

'No. Why? Who is she? What's happened?'

'She is missing. You haven't seen the news?'

'No,' said Robert. 'We have no TV.'

The policeman eyed him suspiciously. 'And you have no passport?'

'No, I've lost it.'

'Where you lose it?'

'I'm not sure but I think it was in my jacket in a bar in the marina.'

The policeman turned away and spoke to someone else who began to fire words into his radio.

'You come to station with us in Portimão.'

The other police officer was still radioing, presumably for back-up. Rob's stomach felt as if it were in a cement mixer but now wasn't a time to crunch up and vomit. That would be a real give-away. He wanted to ask questions but knew he wasn't going to get answers. As he staggered back to the van, he tried to convince himself that it would be all right: he was being allowed to drive, he hadn't been arrested, nor had they breathalysed him. And there was certainly no little girl hidden in the van.

There was no time to call Beks. He followed the police car back into Portimão, past the gypsies, LeClerc, Maxmat and up to the roundabout. This time he turned left towards the police station and the law courts. His stomach whirled around the cement mixer again and his whole body shook as two policemen with hips bulging with guns, batons and handcuffs ushered him into an interview room. This was it. They were going to lock him up and throw away the keys. They indicated to a chair in front of a desk and stood discussing something for what seemed like hours. They didn't even bother speaking to him although, at one point, they clearly made a joke as they both looked at him and laughed. Robert smiled stupidly as if he understood when, really, he might as well be listening to Martian. If he ever got out of this, not only would he never drink again, but he would learn Portuguese. Not understanding a language was like being behind bars.

Someone shouted through the door and one of the officers asked for his van keys. Robert gave them to him. Then, after about half an hour, a short, rotund non-uniformed man hurried in with some folders, his van keys, a litre bottle of water and a plastic bag. The man put the bag on the floor, the water and keys on the table and shuffled the papers around on the desk, while speaking to the other two policemen, all the time, watching Robert. Robert tried to adapt a concerned expression and hide the horror he was feeling. Eventually, the two uniformed officers left.

'Now, Mr Roberte Laysester?' He looked up. 'Is that how you say?'

'Leicester as in Les-ter,' Robert explained, smiling at the rather overweight balding man.

'As in the club, Leicester City?' Robert nodded. 'Ah this English language. How does anyone learn?'

'With difficulty. But not as difficult as Portuguese,' Robert said, warming up. This was turning into a usual exchange.

The man changed his tone, firing at him.

'So, Mr Roberte, where were you exactly last night?'

Robert replied as calmly as he could. 'In Praia de Rocha. I met a guy I know and we went to the casino and then a bar at the marina. And I lost my coat with my passport.'

'And how much did you drink?'

'Three or four *caipirinhas*?' Robert said. 'Too many to drive. I decided to stay in Portimão.'

'So where you sleep?'

Robert sighed. 'At someone's apartment. I'm afraid I only met them last night.'

'Is that why you have sand on your clothes?' the man asked him.

Robert looked down at himself. He had sand on his T-shirt and in the creases of his jeans. Ah shit. He took in a deep breath through an open mouth. Was it illegal to sleep on the beach?

'I walked back to the van along the beach earlier this morning. I sat down for a while and watched the sea.'

'I see. And while you are watching the sea you do not remember to see this girl?' Once again, the image of the blonde girl appeared from out the folder.

Robert shook his head thoughtfully. 'No. There were some people walking a dog but no one suspicious.' Other than me, he thought.

'Okay, then, Mr Roberte.' The man picked up the plastic bag and put it on the table. 'Is this yours?'

Robert was about to deny it but then he saw his black jacket. 'Yes,' he cried out. 'Is my passport in it?' His fingers leapt at the bag, pulled out the jacket and zigzagged over the front in search of the pockets.

'Yes, Mr Roberte, it is there. You are lucky.'

As his fingers felt the passport in the breast pocket, he exhaled slowly, the relief passing through him as if someone had turned on a tap.

'Where did you find it?'

'It was handed in this morning. There was nothing else. You had money?'

'No, I had my wallet with me.'

The inspector looked at the clock on the wall. It was almost eleven o'clock.

'Then, Mr Roberte, you are free to go. But drink this water and, in future, do not drink alcohol and drive. My officers say you stink like a *tasca* this morning.'

4. Beyond the sea

'The sea is already in your blood, son,' his uncle Jorge called to him, smiling, as Mário hopped impatiently by the edge of the sea, waiting for the *Sereia*, his father's boat, to slice through the calm water like a flock of birds from Africa.

His uncle jumped out of the *Fica Bem*, lifted Mário up and swung him into the boat amongst all the ropes and nets and today's catch. The smell of fish made the seagulls squawk and dip above him. Mário swayed from side to side pretending he was at sea. He should be tucked up in bed – he had school soon – but he loved to meet the fishermen coming in from the night's fishing. The sun cast its first white beam onto the water but he still couldn't see the *Sereia*. He wished he were out there chugging through the water, pulling in the nets, sorting out the fish. His father wanted to take Mário with him but his mother wouldn't let him. 'What good will fishing do him?' she'd say. 'I've told him before: he needs to learn to read and write and get a job, not be poor like us.'

Mário didn't care about reading and writing. He wanted to be a fisherman.

'We don't do so bad,' his father would say, rubbing his hand through his hair. 'We have a house, lights, plenty of food, clothes. Times have been much worse. Isn't that right, son?'

Mário would nod while his mother would go on about how much more her sister had being married to a head waiter at the casino in Portimão. His father would grumble that casino waiters worked nights as well – and not just with fish. Mário didn't understand what his father meant but his mother would shut up.

The tractor grumbled to life and chugged down the beach towards them. His uncle put him down on the sand as the other men came to help. Mário shivered in the early morning mist and ran after the tractor as it dragged the boat away from the sea where the tourists swam during the day. Seagulls sat perched on the helm hitching a lift. The red and green paint was chipped but the black letters of *Fica Bem* stretched boldly across the sides while the

54

faded green and red flag flapped around the pole, its yellow centre hidden.

Mário watched in fascination as the nets were untangled and the trays of twitching sea bass and sea bream were passed down. A couple of tourists, clumsy in their big shoes and heavy morning jumpers, nosed around, taking photos. His uncle Jorge didn't look at them, but continued working.

'Any good?' Antonio, the tractor driver, called to his uncle.

'Every time is less but today is not so bad. A swell during the night drove a shoal of sardines almost onto the boat!'

'What luck. Any sign of Rui?'

His uncle pointed out to sea. 'I think that's him over there. There was a flash storm and the sea turned rough for a while. But nothing serious. He'll be in soon.'

Mário followed his uncle's finger to where his father was. If that was him, he was just a speck. Mário felt his eyes smart. He would have to go to school without greeting him. And then he would have to spend the whole day at school. His uncle threw some remains of the catch to the seagulls. They screamed like his little sister.

A basket of crabs was passed down, their clawing legs swimming out of the basket.

'And look at this! I've never seen one so big.'

An octopus the size of a football peered out of a pot, its arms knotted up.

'What a good catch! You will get good money for this.'

'Sometimes the sea gives, sometimes the sea takes,' his uncle said. 'Today it has given.'

On the square his uncle negotiated the fish with the restaurant owners.

'Let's go, Marinho,' his uncle said. 'Your mother will be worried.'

Mário took his uncle's hand and allowed himself to be led up the narrow Rua dos Pescadores to their small house with dark blue borders painted around the door and windows. They met cousin Zé walking down the hill. Cousin Zé was a waiter in the Paraíso, the best restaurant in the village. All his aunts and uncles – and especially his mother, said how well he'd done. He worked inside when the skies were as wet as the sea, he earned good money and had something called a pension which was money he could have when he was an old man. Mário couldn't imagine being an old man, but he could imagine working in a restaurant between four walls and forty tables, constantly rushing around carrying plates of food and drink. Mário didn't want that. He wanted to be on the waves, under the big blue sky on the big blue water.

'Good morning, Zé,' his uncle said.

'Good morning. Hey Marinho.' Zé picked him up, swung him round and put him back down again. Mário felt embarrassed: he was too big to be swung round in the street like a baby. His cousin smelled of cigarettes and *Macieira*. When Mário grew up, he wasn't going to smoke or drink. They made people smell and do silly things. His father didn't drink or smoke any more. He used to but he stopped after the doctor told him that his liver was shrivelled like figs and his lungs were sooted up like the inside of a chimney. The doctor had shown him photos and they now hung on the lounge wall as a reminder. Besides, his father said that many fishermen died when they were drunk. They would drink so much they would fall overboard. A waste of a life, his father would say.

'Did you have a good night?' cousin Zé asked his uncle Jorge.

'Can't complain. Yes, it was a good catch last night. A strange night though. A sudden flash storm at about 3 a.m. and a wind that practically drove a shoal of sardines onto the boat! Very unusual for mid-May.'

'I saw the lightning out at sea in the night,' Zé said.

'Ah so you had a good night, too?' His uncle winked at Zé. 'Who is it? The *bife* teacher who was always waiting for you in the *pastelaria*?'

'No, she's gone. Paulo and I had a few drinks after work. Then we went to a nightclub in Luz but Paulo's crap car broke down so we had to walk back.'

'Walk! My God! Perhaps not a good idea to go to Luz with that trouble. The whole place is cordoned off, isn't it?'

Zé nodded. 'We wanted to see what it was like. The place is swarming with police and TV cameras. But it was okay: the car broke down before we arrived.'

Mário tugged on his uncle's jacket. Everyone was always talking about Luz recently but no one would tell him what had happened. He'd seen photos of a girl on the television but he didn't know what had happened to her.

'So many people have been stopped. You were lucky the car wasn't impounded. Yes, we're going, Marinho.'

'I don't think it would make that much difference. I doubt it will start again. Anyway, sleep well.'

'You too.'

His cousin continued on his way, not quite in a straight line. His uncle banged on their door before opening it.

'Paula, Mário is here,' his uncle called to his mother.

'Ah! I even locked the door and slept on the key so he couldn't get out. I thought he was still in bed.' His mother hit him on the head but it didn't hurt. 'Get ready for school. And don't wake your sister. For once, she's asleep. Go and learn to read and write so that your wife won't have to spend all night worrying about you.'

'But I want to go fishing,' Mário said.

'We'll take you fishing when you're a bit older,' his uncle promised. 'You need to learn to read first. I've told you before: when you can read we'll take you out. Maybe in the summer holidays.'

'He shouldn't be wandering around the beach on his own. Anything could happen to him. Look what happened to that poor little girl in Luz.'

'What happened?' Mário asked.

'No one knows what's happened to her,' his mother said. 'But she disappeared. In the middle of the night. Like you. Only she never came back. Can you imagine the worry of the poor mother? Now go and get changed. And where's my husband this morning?' His mother turned to uncle Jorge. 'I don't see why he always has to be the last one back.'

Mário listened again to the tales of great shoals of fish that had appeared during the night as he put on his school uniform. His uncle left and Mário ate his Nestum and toast. Then he went to school on his own now that he was seven. He passed the group of fishermen huddled together by the nets. A big, green GNR car pulled up and two policemen got out. Mário bet they were looking for treasure. Sometimes, during the night, men came ashore with sacks which they buried in the sand. His father had told him all about it. Or maybe they were looking for the girl who'd disappeared.

Just before he reached the school Mário shimmied up his favourite fig tree from where he could see out to the horizon. He spotted his father's boat getting closer. He lay down in the arms of the tree and imagined what it would be like to be see-sawing over the waves, the boat full of flapping fish, the engine sputtering gently.

At school, Mário read a story about a mermaid who fell in love with a man and gave up being a mermaid to become a girl, even though it was like walking on glass. When the man didn't love her, she threw herself into the sea and disappeared into foam. Maybe that's what happened to the little girl who disappeared in Luz.

Mário ran out of school at lunchtime and saw his uncle Jorge sitting on the kerb under the umbrella of one of the great palm trees. Mário thought it strange as his uncle never came to the school to see him but perhaps his teacher had told him he had learned to read. Perhaps the news had spread. His uncle called to him and got up. Mário ran towards him in excitement.

'Are we going fishing?' Mário said, as his uncle picked him up and kissed him. 'I read a whole story today! I can read!'

'Not today, Marinho.' The dark cracks in his uncle's face had rain in them. He carried him to a point where they could look out to the sea from the cliffs.

'You are too young to understand this, Mário, but sometimes the sea gives. And sometimes it takes.' His uncle's chest shuddered like the boat's engine. 'Last night... it took your father.'

'Where to?' Mário asked, confused.

'To the other side, Marinho.' The engine stuttered again. 'I'm afraid he's not coming back.'

'Why not?'

Mário stared at the sea. It had squiggly marks like his mother's thighs. He gazed at the dark sea and the light horizon and tried to peer over the other side. But he could see nothing but a line. Why would his father not want to come back?

'They found the *Sereia* empty. He must have fallen in the water and drowned.'

'But he doesn't drink.'

'Oh Marinho.' His uncle buried his face into his shoulder and spluttered.

There was some mistake, Mário thought. It was only fishermen who drank that fell in. His uncle had got it wrong. His father hadn't really drowned. Perhaps he had crossed over the horizon to Africa. He imagined sailing out there and over the other side and approaching a golden shore, lined with shipping boats and men pulling in nets, smoking, talking, laughing, watching mermaids at sea. Mário would go there to look for his father. He was sure he would find him.

5. The big doll

Dona Maria gazed at her potatoes. The ground was all churned up. *Caraças!* Those wild pigs again. That was it: after breakfast she would make a big doll to scare them away. She went inside and put on some water to boil just as the telephone rang. She hoped it wasn't her daughter.

'*Mãe*, have you thought about what we said?'

'What was that?' Maria replied, knowing only too well what.

'About moving to Portimão? You can stay with Alicia. She would welcome the company.'

'I don't know, *filha*. Who would look after the vegetables?'

'But, *Mãe*, who's looking after you? There's no one left in the mountains. You are on your own. Now that Jorge has passed away and Zezinha has moved to Monchique, Lúcia to Portimão…'

'Antonio is still here,' Maria said defiantly, even though he and his wife, Ana, still kept themselves to themselves after what had happened to Serafina of the Street.

'Yes, but he's still a way away and you don't speak to him.'

'Well, there's the foreigners,' Maria said. 'They moved in a few weeks ago. I watched them. So many boxes.' She looked out of the window at the newly rebuilt house opposite. There was no sign of them yet, but it was still early. They were young, very glamorous with blond hair. They had been coming to the house since the Day of All Saints, but only after they had put in new windows and doors did they move in. They waved to her everyday and shouted, '*Olá*'. She had taken them her best cabbages and chatted to them. They would smile, but she couldn't understand what they said.

'*Mãe*, they don't even speak Portuguese. How do you talk to them?'

'Well, talk.'

'But they don't understand, do they? Besides they are different. Listen, *Mãe*, I think you should move away. Perhaps sell your house? Zézinha made a fortune selling hers.'

'But it's my home,' Maria said. 'I've lived here all my life.'

'I know *Mãe*, but you're seventy-eight and it is dangerous living on your own. Please think about it.'

Maria thought about it that afternoon as she sat and gazed up at Foía, the still-green summit now spiked with towers and receivers – one of which looked like an ice-cream cone. All around her houses had collapsed in a pile of rubble. It didn't take long. The sun burned like red coals, the rain fell like the devil's piss and the wind howled like a pack of wolves racing down the mountain. And yet, only a few decades ago, the hamlet had been full of families with children shouting and playing, and animals grunting, barking and braying.

It was after the Revolution thing that the world she had known began to disappear: the youngsters went first, declaring that they could make a better living in the towns and cities, then the animals either died or were sold and, finally, her generation limped away – the ones who hadn't already left their boots. Even until last week, Lúcia of the Mill would come and sit with her in the shade of the house. Now, with Lúcia gone, there was no one left. Her daughter was right. But she couldn't live anywhere else – her whole life gazed back at her from these mountains.

Up there, an old trail used to lead to the primary school on the now abandoned terraces of Foía where her daughters used to go to school and, on Sundays, the whole family would go to Mass in Monchique on foot. Two hours it took. They would leave at sunrise and come back before sundown. Sometimes, Maria would get up long before dawn and bake bread to sell in town. They would pack up the donkey and drag him with them.

'It would be easier to pack me up,' her husband used to grumble when the donkey got into one of his moods.

Both she and the donkey would look at him hopefully and they would laugh.

Just above her to the left were the red ruins where they would have the village dance. Everyone used to put on their best and get together. The women would talk, the children play, the men drink *medronho,* and everyone would dance to old Romeo's accordion. As a young woman she had danced with Martinho, her husband – amongst others. You had to be careful in those days, of course. Her older cousin, Serafina of the Street, had done more than dance with Antonio behind the mill. Antonio was the neighbour Maria didn't speak to but, in those days, he was a handsome man who had just come back from Germany with Marks. He had married Ana but she had been ill that night of the *baile*. Serafina had always liked Antonio and must have been seduced by the silver light of the full-moon – or his Marks.

An old enemy of the family had seen them together and threatened to denounce Antonio if he didn't cough up his prize pig. Antonio had gifted the pig, but to make sure the rumours could go no further, Antonio told whoever he could that Serafina of the Street was stealing chickens for the Communists. It was a fox, of course, but no one said anything and Serafina was quietly arrested and taken away one night.

It was years later when Maria heard that Serafina was a maid in Lagos – where she still worked, even though she must be in her eighties. She had never come back to the hamlet. Maria rarely spoke to Antonio or Ana since then, but he had given her a bottle of his *medronho* last Christmas. She supposed it was a long time ago.

These days Antonio was the only one on this side of the mountain who made *medronho* from the wild strawberries. Good thing too. All the men used to make it and it would make their eyes red and blurry and their voice sound like cats. Her husband was always pissed. Once she had gone out to look for him and found his hat on the path while he lay unconscious under a bush. She had left him there. He had even been pissed when he died. They never knew what he had died of but he had insisted on several glasses of *medronho* a day. He'd complained of stomach pains and refused to eat her bread which he said was giving him indigestion. What rubbish. It was more likely the alcohol that killed him.

Even then her daughter had tried to make her go to the city. 'You see, *Mãe*, you don't even have a doctor near here. He might have lived longer if you had.' Maria didn't know if he'd wanted to live longer. She didn't know if she'd wanted him to live longer – God obviously didn't. And, at least, he'd died in their home.

They'd had two daughters who had lived and two sons who had died at birth. She had been lucky to survive herself, apparently, at the stillbirth of her last son. She had bled too much. It was Lúcia's mother who had acted as midwife and saved her life. Of course, that wouldn't happen nowadays, if you lived in a city with hospitals and doctors.

Her daughters, like everyone else's, had left home just as soon as they were able to. They learned to read and write, learned to drive, got jobs, apartments, husbands. One lived in Portimão, the other in

Lisbon. Now their children had grown up and one was in Coimbra, another in Germany. They all lived in cities. She remembered the first time her daughter had taken her to the little box high in the sky in Portimão.

'Everything is clean and civilised,' her daughter said. 'Not like the mountains.'

Maria had stared in wonder at the pretty lights and screens, the shiny tiled floors, the leather sofas, fridges in cupboards, machines that washed clothes, bathrooms with silver taps and soft towels but, after a while, she gazed out the window and at the other blocks of houses and felt trapped. There was no air. And all the earth was covered in concrete. There was nowhere to grow vegetables. Her daughter had laughed at her.

'Why sweat and toil in the countryside when you can go to a shop!'

Maria had tried the vegetables from the shop and, for the first time ever, her *caldo verde* tasted like dirty water, the meat chewy and the chips soggy. Besides, her daughter was getting very fat from going to the shop. Which reminded her: she still needed to make a big doll to scare away the wild boar from her potatoes.

She got up and went around the side of the house to some outbuildings, where she chopped up firewood. She found a couple of long branches and nailed them together. Then she went into her dark kitchen, still smoky from the fire she had made earlier, and took one of the large empty plastic water bottles, which the foreigners threw into the bin everyday, and chopped off the top. She cut holes for three carrots and then more holes around the brim through which she threaded a couple of empty 7-Up cans. In the bedroom she found an old jacket in a chest that had belonged to her husband and an old black cap. She took them outside and dressed the branches in the jacket and then put the big water bottle on top. She slipped some small stones into the 7-Up cans so that they would rattle in the wind and, finally, she tied plastic bags to the hands. As a last touch, she put Martinho's cap on top of the bottle. For a moment she felt tears sting her eyes: even the carrot looked at bit like his nose. Then she carried her big doll across her potato patch and knocked it into the ground along the path between her house and the foreigners'.

'There, Martinho,' she said, 'you scare those pigs.'

She picked some plums and went to sit by the tube next to the water tank to wash them. She would need to irrigate later. She had sixteen hours of irrigation water a week, but now there was no one to look after the tubes. Her daughter didn't seem to think the foreigners would bother, but how could they grow things without water? They would need a lot of bottles.

She heard footsteps behind her and turned round to see the two tall blond people walking towards her, pointing at her doll. They were clearly impressed. She got up and greeted them. 'I was just washing you some plums,' she said. They pumped her hand up and down and said 'good afternoon'. They were almost twice her size and both dressed in blue jeans, sleeveless tops and sturdy leather boots. They could do with being a bit fatter but, otherwise, they were very beautiful. She adjusted her cotton black rimmed hat and patted down her pinafore over her skirt. She would have put on stockings if she'd known they were coming.

'Excuse me, I'm all dusty. Sit down, sit down,' she said, arranging some more stools. They didn't seem to want to, flapping around like giant butterflies, but, eventually, she got them to perch. Ha, she thought, I have new friends! Like angels! I won't have to go to Portimão now. The woman held out her hand and said, 'Bec' or 'Beco'? A dead end? She pointed at the doll again and sliced the air between their land and her land. Did they need access? Confused, Maria told them it was to scare the pigs, the wild boar. The *Senhor* was speaking now, but he wasn't making any sense at all.

'So how do you keep the pigs away in your land?' Maria asked, but she didn't understand their lengthy explanations in their twisted tongues. Then, the *Senhor* produced a book, flicked through it, and showed it to her. It was a nice shiny book, the colour of the sky, but there were no pictures on the page he showed her. Only words. She shook her head, told them she didn't know words and went inside to get some sausage and some of Antonio's *medronho*. She didn't want them to think her rude. She arranged a crate and sat down her best plastic tray with the bottle and glasses, slices of *chouriço* and bread – sadly, not freshly baked – and poured the *medronho*. The man tried to say 'no' but Maria insisted.

'To new neighbours!' Maria said, holding up a glass.

They clinked glasses, drank the *medronho* and smiled – well, grimaced. But that was normal with the first glass.

Maria picked up the plate of sausage and offered it to them. They shook their heads. Maria said it was good *chouriço,* but they still wouldn't take any. She tried to offer more *medronho* but they didn't want any more of that either. They took the plums though and left saying, 'good afternoon' and 'thank-you'. The *Senhora* pointed again to the doll and put her hands together as if in prayer. Maybe she wanted one? But they weren't growing anything. Anyway, it was right in front of their house so it would scare the pigs for them. She took the tray back into the kitchen with a heavy heart. At least, they had visited her.

After she had emptied the tank onto her land and made sure that the water was running through the channels, she went into her house and looked for her phone book. She found her daughter's photograph and dialled the number.

'I'm glad you called, *Mãe*. Have you thought about what we talked about this morning? I have an estate agent who can come to look at your house whenever you want.'

'What's an estate agent?' Maria asked.

'Someone who sells houses.'

'I don't know, *filha*.' She paused. 'The foreigners came to visit me today.'

'That's nice. What did you talk about?'

'Hm. Not much.'

'No?'

'No, it was very strange. I offered them some *chouriço* and they wouldn't eat it.'

'Perhaps they just had lunch?'

'It was late in the afternoon.'

'Well, perhaps they're vegetarians.'

'Veger what?'

'Vegetarians. You know, people who don't eat meat.'

'Don't eat meat? There are people who don't eat meat?'

'Lots of foreigners don't, *Mãe*. I told you they were different. They don't like to kill animals.'

'Well, what do they do with them then?'

'I don't know. They probably don't have any, do they?'

'No.'

'It's also for health reasons. I bet they're not fat, are they?'

'No,' Maria said. Maybe her daughter should be one of these veger-whatsits. 'So what should I cook them for lunch?'

'Vegetables?'

'Just vegetables? But they will think I am mean.'

'No, they won't. Just cook some vegetables with tomatoes or something.'

Maria ate some soup which she made the previous day and then went into the living room. On the sideboard decorated with lace, which her mother had crocheted when she was younger, there was a black and white picture of herself and Martinho, her mother and their two daughters, about fifty years ago outside the house. The donkey was in the background. The little bugger.

She switched on the television. She could live perfectly well without those machines that wash and cook, but she couldn't imagine life without a television. Whoever had thought of being able to send pictures through a box should be made a saint. Her daughters had bought it for her after her husband died fifteen winters ago. A good companion, as it turned out, especially as she had been the first to have one and the neighbours used to come round to watch it.

The evening news was still on. Pictures of that pretty little girl who had disappeared filled the screen. The parents were coming out of a church holding a flower. They were very handsome, like her new neighbours – tall, blonde, with sky-blue eyes sad as a puppy's, but the mother wasn't wailing and crying. It was because she was English, they said. And a doctor. Maria couldn't imagine being able to hold all that pain inside. Poor lady. Poor child. Who could have taken her? More than a month had passed. Who could have done such a thing to a little girl? It didn't bear thinking about. Maria switched over to watch *Dança Comigo* where Cecilia from *Ilha dos Amores* was waltzing. She whirled, twirled, stopped and spun around the man like a dragonfly. She should win.

Early the next morning Maria got up and, after taking some tomatoes out of the freezer, she went down to her potato patch. It didn't look like the pigs had been in the night. There had been a wind and the cans had been jingling all night, making a right racket. Ha! she thought, satisfied, her big doll had worked. 'You see, Martinho, you made yourself useful at last.' She dragged some branches to her door and chopped them up for the fire. She lit it and put on a pot of water to boil. Then she went back outside and prepared to spray her vegetables. She loaded the chemicals on her back and sprayed her cabbages and beans. That done, she picked a courgette and some beans – they were almost ready.

It was already hot as she went inside and made herself a cup of coffee and ate some toast. The bits got in between her false teeth so she had to take them out and clean them. She washed her face, combed her grey hair, slipped a slide in her fringe and put on her hat. Then she went into the kitchen, added some more wood to the fire and began chopping up vegetables. Even with the fire going, the dark kitchen was cool compared to the fire outside. Her daughters used to tell her to have the floor tiled, but she liked it as it was. It kept the kitchen cool. She had tiles in the other rooms. And lights of course, and hot water in the bathroom. Her husband had even arranged a shower many years ago by hanging up a bucket with holes in it. Her daughter wanted to have a proper shower installed, but Maria liked the bucket. It reminded her of Martinho.

When the vegetables were simmering away, she went outside into the yellow sun and up the path towards the foreigners' house, greeting Martinho on the way. Many years ago their house had belonged to her parents, but they had given it to her uncle in return for a spring. Their grandchildren had sold it last year. They all thought they were going to be rich, but Maria heard that by the time they divided it all up between the seven of them, paid the person who sold the house, and solicitors, there had hardly been anything left. Not that there had been much left of the house either. But it faced the sun, and now it was shining white. Her mother had told her she had been born there. She didn't remember of course, but she remembered climbing the old fig tree in front with her cousins.

'Good morning,' she called out.

The *Senhora* was painting around the doors and windows. Her husband appeared from out of the kitchen with two cups in his hand. Martinho had never made her coffee.

'Good morning,' the *Senhora* said. She had a splash of blue paint on her cheek. The same colour as her eyes.

'I've made you lunch if you want. Only vegetables, I'm afraid, as my daughter said that you were veger-somethings.'

'I'm sorry I don't understand,' the *Senhora* replied.

Maria spoke louder.

'Lunch?' the *Senhora* repeated.

Maria nodded her head vigorously and indicated that they come with her, but they were gibbering away to each other. They shook their heads and said 'Sorry' and 'Monchique'.

'Ah well, never mind, another time.'

The *Senhora* was pointing at her big doll again.

66

'You see, it worked! No pigs!' Maria said, triumphantly.

She thought that the *Senhora* said that it made a lot of noise. Maria nodded, pleased. 'Just like my husband used to!' she added, but she didn't think the *Senhora* understood as she frowned and went back to painting the doors.

'I'm sorry to bother you, then,' Maria said. 'Perhaps another time. Good afternoon to you.'

Maria went back to the pot of boiling vegetables and went to cut some bread but she couldn't find the bread knife. She sawed at it with a small vegetable knife instead. She would have that and the *chouriço*. She sat down in her kitchen to eat with her door open. The jeep and van were still there. They were still there when she washed the dishes. Maybe they had changed their mind. She put the lid on the saucepan and headed once again up the path. A hot wind was blowing. The cans on the big doll rattled noisily. *Caraças.* If the wind picked up it could burn the cabbages.

'I've bought you some lunch in case you don't go to town,' she called out, but she couldn't see anyone. She cupped her hand around the glass and peered in. The *Senhora* was sitting on some bags of cement in front of a computer. Maria knocked on the door to get her attention. Her eyes looked tired when she opened the door.

'I've brought you some lunch in case you don't go to town,' Maria said again and handed her the pan. The *Senhora* looked doubtful.

'Vegetarian,' she said.

'It's just vegetables.' Maria lifted the pot to show her.

The *Senhora* smelled the food and her eyes smiled.

'Thank-you, thank-you.'

'Nothing,' Maria said. 'It's nothing much. Well then, see you later.'

The door shut behind her and she went back to her house. She would have a little watch of *Ilha dos Amores* and a nap. Then, when it was cooler, she would pick the cucumbers and lettuces. She must remember to take the chicken out the freezer and prepare the yeast. Her daughter and son-in-law would arrive first thing in the morning. As she put her hand in the freezer, she felt something slice. Her finger burned. She peered into the freezer and saw the bread knife gleaming up at her. She whipped her hand out and found blood dripping from her finger. *Caraças!* She must have left the knife in there when she was opening the bag of tomatoes. She rushed outside and stuck her finger in the running water. The water ran red. She ripped off a piece of cloth from her apron and tied it round, hoping that it would stop the flow. She went inside to find a bandage, but she couldn't find one so she ripped up a large pair of knickers. She removed the soaked piece of apron and poured a little *medronho* over the cut. Then tied it up again.

'*Mãe,* let me look, what have you done to your hand?'

Her daughter had only just landed in the kitchen and already she was on at her, telling her she couldn't look after herself, what if she had fallen?

'I didn't fall. I just cut my finger on a knife yesterday and it opened up during the night. Now I will have to wash the sheets.'

'Let me have a look. Why didn't you put a bandage on?'

'I couldn't find one.'

'Why didn't you ask your new neighbours?' her daughter continued in a yappy, official voice as she unwrapped the strips of cotton knickers. Her daughter worked at the Health Centre in Portimão and was used to shouting at people. 'It's a deep cut.'

'I didn't like to bother them.'

'You see?' her daughter said, knowingly. 'Wait here. I've got some antiseptic cream in the car.'

Her daughter cleaned the cut, smeared on some antiseptic cream and applied a proper bandage. João, her son-in-law, set to work lighting a fire in the bread oven. Maria sat in the dark kitchen with her throbbing finger while her daughter rolled the dough.

'I saw Lúcia the other day,' her daughter said.

'How is she?' Maria knew what her daughter was going to say and she was determined not to fall into the trap.

'She's loving it. She goes to Mass, visits her friends…'

'That's nice,' Maria said.

'Yes. She says she's never been happier.'

Maria was puzzled. Lúcia would never say that, would she? She went outside to see if the fire was burning well. João was adding more sticks.

'Almost ready,' he said.

Her daughter came out with a tray carrying the lumps of dough which she shovelled into the oven. She then scrubbed the sheets as well as doing some of her own washing from Portimão. Even her daughter said that the machines couldn't get the clothes as clean as the fresh mountain water and sun. Then they spent the rest of the

morning digging, pruning, fertilizing. Maria picked some beans –
while her daughter prepared the chicken *piri-piri*.

'I'm going to take the foreigners some bread,' Maria said. 'They
haven't used their bread oven yet.'

'I bet they won't like it,' her daughter said. 'They like soft
bread.'

What rubbish, Maria thought, as she took out the batch of loaves,
the smell of freshly baked bread and charcoal gusting from the
oven. Everyone liked her bread – well, except for Martinho when
he was dying, but he didn't count. She knocked on each loaf and
returned a couple that weren't quite ready. The rest she took into
the kitchen. She wrapped one in a cloth and then she walked up to
the house. There was no one around, but both the jeep and van
were still there. Maria peered in through the windows but couldn't
see anyone so she banged on the door. The lady appeared in a
dressing gown.

'I'm sorry to trouble you but I have brought you some bread.'
Maria lifted the cloth to show her the bread.

'Bread?' she replied, smiling. 'Oh thank-you.'

'It is not the best loaf I have ever made – it's hard to keep the
oven hot enough – but it's not too bad.'

'Thank you.'

'Well I mustn't keep you.'

Maria walked away. The door shut behind her. Where the land
hadn't been watered, the grass had turned to straw and the earth
had shrivelled to crumbs. At least the wind hadn't picked up
during the night.

'They are still sleeping?' her daughter asked.

'Yes,' Maria said. 'They work late.'

At one o'clock, they all sat down on the stools in the shade of the
fig tree to chicken *piri-piri*, chips, salad and the freshly baked
bread and olive oil. João opened a bottle of red wine and Maria got
some cans of 7-Up to add to it.

'The foreigners are off out,' Joao said. 'Nice car. An almost new
Discovery.'

They were getting into the white jeep.

'See you later!' Maria shouted, waving to them from the table.

They waved back.

'She's very attractive,' her daughter said.

'Yes,' Maria said. 'He's not bad either.'

'Do they have children?'

'Not yet,' Maria said. 'It will be nice when they do.'

As they were washing the dishes, her daughter began again. Maria took a deep breath.

'But *Mãe,* it is dangerous to stay here on your own. There is no one here to help you. You are forgetful and I don't want you to hurt yourself.'

'I won't hurt myself,' Maria said, angry that her daughter was treating her like a child.

'What about the knife?'

'That was an accident.'

'Exactly.'

'Don't you want to have friends around you?'

Maria felt her will ebbing and before they left she agreed that they could come and pick her up on Wednesday evening and she would stay with Alicia, Joao's sister, who was now on her own since Zé died. In return, they promised that they would bring her back every weekend. Maria sighed as she switched on the television. She took off her old boots which Martinho had got her about a year before he died. She wouldn't be needing them for much longer. She knew she would die in that concrete box in the sky.

Wednesday dawned and despite the blue skies and the early morning shadows on the green mountains, Maria felt a deep sadness. She cleaned the house and took a single plastic bag of rubbish to the bins.

She went back to her land, picked up an *enxada* and dug a patch at the end of the bottom terrace she hadn't used for planting since Martinho died. She was soon sweating as the sun rose above the mountains and had to stop. She peeled an orange and sat in the shade of the fig tree and closed her eyes, ignoring the fly buzzing around her.

'Good morning.'

Maria opened her eyes to see the *Senhora,* flickering above her like a vision. She sat up and blinked.

'Lunch?' the *Senhora* said.

'Lunch?' Maria repeated.

'Yes. We make. Here. One o'clock. Is that good?' The *Senhora* tapped her watch.

'That's good,' Maria said, confused.

The vision disappeared. But they were coming to lunch! And she had learned to speak. Perhaps she wouldn't have to die in a concrete box after all. There was hardly any time. Maria had only just put the potatoes in the fat when the neighbours appeared in the doorway with a saucepan.

'Hi, I bring lunch,' the *Senhora* said, showing her the contents of the saucepan.

The *Senhor* stood there holding a bottle of red wine and some strange looking brown bread with seeds on it.

Maria looked at the steaming rice and vegetable dish with aubergines. It smelled of coriander, her favourite.

'And I'm making some chips and some salad.' She poured olive oil over the lettuce.

'Outside?' the *Senhora* asked her.

'I don't mind. We can eat inside if you like? It's cooler.'

But they were already heading towards the table under the fig tree. The *Senhor* had found glasses and knives and forks and was taking them to the table. He then gathered some stools. Maria shook her head. Her husband had never done that in his life. She looked over to the big doll and said, 'You see, what other men do!' She took the chips out of the pan and tipped them onto a plate. Despite her protestations, the *Senhor* carried them and some plates outside. Within seconds the table was laden with food and drink and her two angels were perched there looking at her expectantly.

'Eat, eat!' Maria cried. 'You need to be fatter!'

But they were holding up their glasses to her.

'To neighbours!' they said.

'To neighbours,' she said, smiling. Her daughter was wrong; they weren't different, they were her friends.

She tried the aubergine dish. It needed salt, but it wasn't bad. She didn't much like the bread: it had so many seeds and it hardly had a crust. Fortunately, she had a little piece of chicken *piri-piri* left over which she could have later.

After they had eaten, Maria told them that she had to go to Portimão to live. But she would come back. Perhaps she could come back to live one day. Perhaps she could persuade her daughter that she would be all right now.

'You go away? To Portimão? Forever?' the *Senhora* asked again.

Maria shrugged. It wouldn't be forever. The apartment was in the sky but it was definitely not heaven. But for a while. A few weeks perhaps.

'What a shame,' the *Senhora* said, her blue eyes as open as windows. 'Then can we take?' she asked, pointing to her big doll.

Maria wondered where they wanted to put it but, of course, she said yes. The eyes smiled at her. She asked them to make sure they put it back when they were finished with it because the pigs may still come and eat her vegetables but they were gabbling to each other in their twisted tongues.

As soon as they'd gone, she called her daughter.

'You needn't come as I have new friends,' she shouted.

But her stubborn daughter insisted and they arrived exactly when she said she would.

Her new friends waved to her as she sat quietly in the back of the car. They were so beautiful. As the car went past their house, she peered through the rear window and saw Martinho's arms waving at her as the foreigners pulled him out and took him towards a pile of rubble and broken glass. Strange, she thought, the pigs wouldn't go there. She watched silently as the big doll was thrown down onto an old broken door. Martinho's nose hit a bottle and fell off, and his black hat rolled into the dust. She almost smiled before closing her eyes as the car began to snake through the mountains, towards the city built of boxes by the sea.

6. Vida

Charlotte leaned out of her bed and rippled open the shutters of their fourth floor Portimão apartment a fraction so that white light blasted through the holes. She blinked and threw the sheet over her head – even after three months she still wasn't used to the intensity of the light, about eight thousand times of that outside her flat in Chelsea. She found her mobile. She'd had to switch it off at about 5 a.m. as Ed wouldn't stop texting her. Unlike Rodrigo. It immediately beeped three messages and she laughed out loud. He just wouldn't give up. Today's messages (or rather last night's) were: 'Are you asleep yet? I enjoyed tonight very much. xxx', 'Did I tell you that you are the most gorgeous girl I have ever met? xxx', 'You are. Goodnight. xxx'. The phone vibrated in her hand and another text came through. 'Are you awake yet babe? How about I take you and the girls out on a boat?' She giggled, shook her head and glanced at the time. 12.30 p.m.. She could hear either Vicky or Sarah making noises in the kitchen. A voice like Shakira's was singing about it being illegal to break a woman's heart – it was Sarah.

She threw back the sheet, sat up, ripped up the shutters halfway and squinted into the blinding light until she could see the triangle of glittering turquoise through a gap in the Portimão buildings. She slipped her feet into her blue and white Neilson flip-flops and her arms into a pale blue silk dressing gown with finely stencilled butterflies that Rodrigo had bought her from Japan, and flip-flopped on the terracotta tiles to the bedroom door.

Sarah was outside the door, still singing, holding a mug of tea.

'Hey, Charlotte. Here you are.'

'You're such a sweetie, thank you.'

'So Charlotte,' Vicky called from the lounge. 'Where's Ed taking us today?'

Charlotte laughed as she and Sarah went to join Vicky, who was lying on the black leather sofa in her pink camisole and a pair of lace knickers. Gucci sunglasses swept her hair away from her face

73

and a copy of the Daily Mail lay sprawled across her belly. Vicky was three years older than Charlotte, twenty-nine, but still looked and danced great.

'Well, we've been invited on a boat trip,' Charlotte said, sitting down on one of the black chairs.

'Fantastic,' Sarah said, clapping her hands. 'I love boats!'

'Whereabouts?'

'I don't know. I haven't replied. What am I going to do?' Charlotte said, stretching her long legs out to the coffee table, admiring her carmine toenails.

'Call him and find out!' Vicky replied.

'No, you idiot, what am I going to do about *him*?'

'What's there to do? He's just a nice guy. You're not doing anything wrong, are you?'

'No,' Charlotte said. 'But we did kiss last night.' She hadn't wanted to bring him up to the apartment, afraid of what might happen, so they had lingered in the shadows, heating up the sodium-lit street, a green *Farmácia* cross on a white background in front of them. Then, he had pulled her towards him. It was inevitable, he said, as he kissed her. His lips were warm, soft, undemanding. She held his head in her hands and kissed him back. Their bodies had moved closer together, pressing tighter and tighter as if locking themselves together. She had had to fight to release herself, telling him that she couldn't.

'Sweet!' Sarah said.

'Then what?' Vicky asked, grinning.

'I told him for the thousandth time that it wasn't a good idea, that I was married, and that I loved my husband. The same shit I've been telling him for the last three weeks.'

'What did he say?'

'He said he couldn't understand how anyone married to me could leave me alone for more than a day.'

The other two girls fell silent, hugging their mugs of tea. The strange thing was as soon as Charlotte said it, she worried that it might be true. But it couldn't be. Rodrigo was a footballer – he needed to train every day. He'd just been signed up by Milton Keynes Dons, a League Two team but Rodrigo was sure they were heading up. He hadn't wanted her to take this job: they didn't need the money, they had a nice flat in Chelsea. About a month after they were married, Rodrigo had said she should stop dancing; she had already danced for twenty years – wasn't that enough? So she had quit the West End show she had danced in for two years. The first couple of months had been a holiday, but then she began to get bored – and fat. What was the point of training to be a dancer since she was five if she wasn't going to dance? She was only twenty-six.

So when this opportunity arose, she had been determined to take it. It was only for eight months, it was in Portugal, Rodrigo could fly out for a couple of days whenever he wanted. And he was Brazilian so he even spoke the same language – although he had lived in the UK since he was eleven. She told him it was something she really wanted to do. Eventually, he'd agreed. They spoke most days, he was working hard and she was, well, having the time of her life. This was the best dancing job she'd ever had. Rodrigo kept saying he was coming to visit but hadn't made it yet. In fact, he hadn't even called her yesterday.

Her mobile vibrated in her hand again. She thought it might be Rodrigo, but it was Ed again. She read the new text out, conscious of a grin pushing the boundaries of her flushed cheeks.

'How about I pick you all up at 2.00 p.m. and we go for a cruise, a swim from the boat, a tiny glass of champagne and oysters? xxx'

The girls shrieked.

'He's got a boat?' Sarah asked, spilling her tea on the sofa. 'Fantastic!'

'I don't think so,' Charlotte said, scrolling up the message again to check that she hadn't misread it. 'Maybe he means a tourist boat.'

'Even so,' Sarah said. 'That would be great fun. What do you reckon, girls? I've never been on a boat. Come on, let's get ready. It's Friday and we don't have a rehearsal this afternoon. We can take a change of clothes with us in case we need to go straight to work. Vicky?'

'Oh, I'm in. It's up to Charlotte. She's the one who has to fight off prince charming.'

'More like the old king,' Charlotte said. 'He's twelve years older than me.'

'Well, you've already got a younger one,' Vicky said.

She smiled as she said it, but Charlotte was getting the impression that Vicky was none too impressed with her marriage to Rodrigo.

'Okay, let's get ready, girls.'

'I'm ready,' Sarah called as they all gracefully unfolded themselves and went to their rooms.

At two, Ed's dark head and puppy eyes appeared on the security cameras. Charlotte told him they'd be down in a second. A second later, they were piling into his yellow Land Rover Defender that Sarah had already christened 'Mustard', bags over their shoulders, sunglasses in place and hair drifting across faces in the breeze that whipped between the apartment blocks.

'Hey girls, are you ready for the best afternoon of your lives?'

Charlotte smiled at him while Sarah yipped. This was the first time Sarah had been out of England, everything was new to her. She was a good dancer: too good for the show, Charlotte thought, as she climbed in the front, but Sarah, like many of them, had wanted the job because it took them to other worlds – without resorting to cruise boats. Vegas was the other popular destination but there was a lot more stripping involved. Charlotte didn't mind in *Vida* – it was part of the story representing reproduction and life and, besides, it was only the top part. There were thousands of tits on the beaches. What was the difference? But she didn't think she could do the Vegas shows.

Charlotte found herself looking at Ed in amazement. His smooth lightly tanned skin, gleaning slightly from sun-cream, looked like that of a child's rather than a thirty-eight-year-old's. It had been a good idea to shave off his goatee beard and moustache and his hair was now spiky but not crew-cut as it was when she met him. He never ceased to surprise her. In three weeks he had taken them surfing, to numerous beaches, driven them up to the Monchique mountains for lunch and bounced them around the little mountain tracks in Mustard. They had seen eagles, snakes and he had told them tales of how he had been looking at a ruin and come face to face with a wild boar and had to run for his life. He had taken them for drives after work up into the hills and shown her shooting stars and Orion. He had dined them at expensive restaurants in Alvor and Portimão, always ordering fresh fish and the best wines – even though they couldn't drink much before work. He had presented them with flowers after a performance – red roses for her, pink and white roses for Sarah and Vicky. They had drunk champagne all night on the sofas on the beach at Nikki's. One rainy afternoon, he had taken them to the shopping centre and cinema at Guia and had bought them all ear-rings, lapis lazuli – a beautiful sky-blue stone – for her, 'to go with her eyes', he had told her. He was almost too good to be true.

His hand slipped from the steering wheel onto her tanned legs. Behind her, Sarah and Vicky were yelling about the next Nikki beach night at full moon. Jon J would be DJing.

'Are you all right?' he said in carefully articulated English. Sometimes his public school past gave him away but mostly the fifteen years he had spent in New York and California had left him with an American accent that Charlotte found refreshing. He lifted his sunglasses and looked at her. There was concern in his eyes, as if he really did care. He stroked her leg gently before returning to the steering wheel.

'Yeah, of course,' she said, smiling. 'I was just thinking.'

'About me, I hope.'

'Yeah,' she said.

'At last!' he yelled, grinning, whipping round a corner so fast that Sarah and Vicky had to hold on. Bottles of champagne twirled around the floor. They shouted at him to be careful.

'Where's the boat, anyway?' Charlotte asked, seeing that they were heading to the 125 and not the Portimão marina.

'Lagos.'

'Is it yours?'

'No, it belongs to a friend of mine, Pedro. There's the five of us going out.'

'Excellent,' Charlotte said, dangling one arm out of the window and breathing in the afternoon Portimão scents of coffee and almond tarts. Life in the Algarve, she decided, was good. Very good.

They arrived into Lagos singing 'Mama Mia'. Sarah had been in the stage performance last year and as Ed only had a strange collection of jazz they preferred to sing. A circus was parked on the wasteland before the roundabout. Charlotte could see llamas and elephants in makeshift pens. There was a big poster of a man with a moustache and a tiger leaping through a hoop. He looked like he'd jumped out of the last century – or even the one before.

'Hey, we could go to the circus one day,' she called.

'You bet,' Ed said. 'I was going to suggest it but you Brits are so sensitive about animals in circuses.'

'Why?' said Charlotte.

'Because you think it's cruel. But what would you rather be doing: crawling through the Sahara looking for water or bowing to an audience and given a cool bath every day?'

She shrugged. 'I'd rather be going out in a boat and drinking champagne.'

Ed laughed. She liked it when she made him laugh. He turned at the roundabout, around Pingo Doce, a supermarket, and parked at the back of the marina. They all piled out of Mustard. Charlotte smoothed down her blue shorts, the same shade as her eyes, and threw her matching blue Harrod's bag (a birthday present from Rodrigo) over her shoulder. Ed found a bag for the champagne.

Pedro appeared from a restaurant, a cigarette hanging out of his mouth and carrying a bucket and a beer. He was bigger then the average Portuguese man but still shorter than they were. He was good looking with his sun-streaked dark hair and those sea-green eyes that Charlotte had noticed all over the Algarve. Rows of blue and white boats tinkled happily as they rested by the pontoons. Charlotte wondered which one they were going on. Pedro greeted Ed like a long lost friend and shook hands with all of them. Then he spoke to Ed before disappearing round the corner of the marina.

'Where's he gone?' Charlotte asked.

'To sort the boat out. It's moored at Cais M – the other side. He reckons we should eat something light before setting off.'

'What about the oysters?' Vicky asked cheekily.

'Well, apparently they're not quite oysters but I'm told we will love them,' Ed said and winked at Charlotte. 'But still better to eat something first.'

They sat down in the shade at one of the outside tables in front of the tinkling boats and ordered fresh orange juice and sandwiches. Ed paid of course and, after they had eaten, he led them round the marina, past a sailing centre to Cais M. Pedro came and swiped his pass to let them in and they clattered along the floating pathways to the black rubber boat called 'Storm'.

The girls laughed when they saw it. It looked like a big dinghy.

'Do not laugh,' Pedro said. 'This is an ex-military Rigid Raidor. Fastest boat in this marina.'

'So we don't have to row?' Vicky said, smiling. She was looking good in her Gucci sunglasses, a floppy sunhat and a wrap-around skirt that could be quickly unwrapped. Her blond hair, washed and left to dry, shone in the sun.

'No, you don't have to row – too much.' Pedro winked at Vicky, caressing her with a smile.

Charlotte smiled. Vicky hadn't had much luck with men. She had never been married, had had a series of crap boyfriends and a string of unpleasant dates here in the Algarve. One guy from Albufeira had taken her out for dinner one night, then waited for the show to end in order to escort her back to a hotel he'd booked. Vicky, politely but firmly, refused to get in the taxi with him. And then there was that idiot, Robert, Ed had met a couple of months ago, who wouldn't leave her alone all night. When they'd tried to escape, he'd grabbed hold of Vicky's bag and wouldn't give it back until she got in the taxi with him. In the end, they had all got in, saying that they were going to a party on the beach and left him there as he started walking in circles looking at the stars.

Pedro helped them onto the boat and they seated themselves along the columns of seats, with instructions to hold onto the rails in front of them. Ed put the champagne into a cool-box and lifted up one of the seats to put the box in. Pedro removed the tarpaulin that covered the console near the back of the boat, then handed out orange life-jackets.

'Must we?' Vicky asked.

'Of course not. If you are good swimmer.'

The girls put them on as the Yamaha roared to life.

'Today is quite calm, we should be fine.'

Pedro reversed away from the pontoon, another beer in his hand. Charlotte thought it amazing how many beers Portuguese men could drink during a day. She looked behind her at Ed, who stood next to him, arms folded. He hadn't put on his life-jacket but he was already amply padded so he could probably float for days. She smiled to herself.

The boat slipped out of Lagos marina, under the footbridge, past the sentinel palm trees. Hundreds of people walked or cycled next to the riverside on the Avenida; many with dogs, pushchairs and children in tow, others sat on the wall and lazily watched the sweltering July afternoon slip by. Seagulls glided like paper aeroplanes as if too hot to flap their wings. Further out, Charlotte gazed at Meia Praia stretching all the way to Alvor in one crescent strip of gold. Not a single white blemish dusted the sky.

'Hold on girls,' Pedro called.

Ed just had time to sit next to her before the boat leapt forward, throttling noisily, and headed out to the horizon. Sarah was shrieking and they all grinned helplessly as the boat jumped on top of the waves. Ed slipped his arm around her and, before she'd even thought about it, she snuggled up to him. Sarah and Vicky were waving at other passengers on other boats.

'You okay?' he asked her.

'I'm great.'

She was. She couldn't help thinking that this was the happiest time of her life. Pedro slowed down to show them the Ponte de Piedade and the lighthouse perched on top. He also showed them the rock formations – the camel's head, the chimney and the devil's eye. He was going to take them into the caves but it was crowded with boats so they sped out towards Africa, flying above the waves.

At last, he slowed down and cut the engine so that they rocked in silence on the undulating seascape while the waves washed the boat.

'Time for some refreshment, I think,' Ed said, going to the cool box for a bottle of champagne.

He handed them all plastic cups and popped the bottle open. It was Veuve Cliquot.

'We shouldn't. We have a show this evening,' Vicky half-heartedly said, taking a sip. 'Yum! Cheers Ed, Cheers Pedro, cheers girls. Another wonderful day.'

They held their cups up, trying not to fall over to reach each other. Pedro practically snorted his cup.

'Love it,' Sarah said, leaning over the side and dipping her fingers in the water. 'Can we swim here?'

'Probably best not here. We are long way from coast. We stop on the way back.'

'So do you do this all the time, Pedro?' Vicky asked.

'Ah yes, I am big playboy.' He winked at her. 'No, I am fisherman and I do tourist trips like this.'

Pedro produced the bucket he had taken on board earlier. 'These are *percebes,* barnacles. Just like oysters. You eat like this.' He demonstrated how to eat one, taking it out of its shell, and they all tried.

'Yuck!' Vicky said. 'They're nothing like oysters! More like spotted slugs.'

For once, Sarah found something she didn't love so much. Charlotte didn't mind them but Vicky was right about the slugs. Ed couldn't stop eating them and opened another bottle of champagne. As they sat there drinking they saw a circle of ripples on the waves as if a big hairdryer was blowing onto the surface.

'Dolphins feeding,' Pedro said.

'Dolphins! I've never seen dolphins in the sea,' Sarah said.

Neither had Charlotte. She looked at the churned up patch of water excitedly.

Pedro yanked the engine back to life and they bounced very slowly towards the rippling cauldron. Every so often a slim hump of a dolphin arched in and out of the circle.

'There they are!' Sarah shouted.

'They circle the shoals of fish so they can't get away. Then they eat them.'

Vicky slipped them some *percebes* when Pedro wasn't looking. Charlotte laughed.

On the way back Ed put his arm around her and they snuggled up together. He kissed her forehead, then her cheek, then her lips. She knew the others were watching but she didn't care. Pedro showed them Luz bay and told them that was where the little girl was kidnapped.

'The boat wait here and then take her to Spain or, perhaps, Morocco.'

'How do you know?' Vicky asked. 'Was it you?'

Pedro laughed. 'No, not me. But I think that what happens. So many smuggling boats in these waters.'

Charlotte didn't say anything. Everyone had their own theory.

Sarah wanted to go swimming so Pedro stopped off in a bay where the water was a deep dark turquoise and as smooth as a plate. Ed held onto his nose and rolled backwards from the boat into the water. Charlotte gasped. Sarah pulled down her shorts and lifted off her T-shirt, then slipped into the sea, screaming, making more turbulence in the water than the dolphins.

'It's freezing!' she cried.

'Come on, Charlotte,' Ed yelled, floating on his back like a big eiderdown.

Charlotte dipped her fingers in – it was freezing.

'Vicky?'

'No way.' Vicky and Pedro lit cigarettes and sat smoking peacefully. Pedro swigged another beer.

Charlotte slowly stepped out of her blue shorts and took off her T-shirt. She was wearing her favourite light blue and black bikini from Next. She sat on the edge of the boat, swung her legs round and pushed herself in. The cold hit her harder than a shot of tequila. She gasped as she trod water, trying very hard to tread out.

'It's lovely once you get used to it,' Sarah called.

Charlotte swam over to Ed and tried to use him as a cushion but they both sank. Pedro threw them some snorkels and they put them on. Charlotte put her head into the other world and forgot about the cold as she saw the underwater castles of rock guarded by shoals of black and electric blue fish. Ed swam next to her, every so often stroking her stomach, making her quiver. They were quite a long way from the boat when his fingers slipped beneath her bikini.

By the time they got back to Lagos, it was already six o'clock and Ed drove them straight to the casino. They could shower and change there. Charlotte noticed her phone had three missed calls registered from Rodrigo. Typical. He hadn't called her for two days and then he called her three times the few hours she was out at sea. Charlotte wanted to speak to him but not while Ed was still around so she switched her phone off. Just as soon as Ed had dropped them off at Praia de Rocha, she switched it back on and it rang immediately. It was him.

'Hey Rod, how's things?' she said coolly.

'I've been trying to call you all afternoon. Where are you, Charlotte?' he said.

'I'm at the casino now, why?'

'Well, you didn't return my calls. Where've you been?'

'The girls and I went out on a boat today and I didn't hear the phone – or maybe there was no signal out at sea. Sorry.'

'Oh,' he said. 'You didn't tell me.'

'No, how would I tell you? You didn't call me yesterday. I'm telling you now. It was a fantastic trip. And you, are you okay?'

'Yeah, I'm fine. A bit tired. We had an eight-hour training session yesterday.'

'Did it go well?'

'Yeah. We won against Chelsea in a friendly on Monday night in the new stadium.'

'That's great.'

'Yes, the new manager is making a difference. I think we'll go places next season.' He paused. 'How's the dancing?'

'It's all good. Everything is great. I love it here. You should come over.'

'I should.'

'Good. Listen I have to go and get ready. Call me tomorrow, Rod. Okay?'

'Charlotte?'

'What?'

'I'm here. In the Algarve. I'm outside your apartment. I wanted to surprise you.'

'What? You are fucking joking?'

'No, I'll come to the show, then take you out afterwards. I've booked us into the Oriental.'

Charlotte felt like the boat had overturned and she was floundering beneath it as she heard herself say 'okay' before snapping shut her phone. She shook herself and ran to the dressing rooms. The girls looked at her expectantly. 'Rodrigo's here, Rodrigo's here,' she said, almost hysterically. 'What am I going to do? He's booked into the same hotel as Ed!' Their mouths fell open before forming multiple questions, most of which she couldn't answer. She didn't know when he'd arrived or how long he was staying. She didn't know how she felt about him being here. She didn't know how she felt about Ed. Ed, Ed. She must text him and let him know.

By the time her make-up and hair was done and she was ready for the show, her stomach was in knots. She regretted eating those slugs. Even the champagne felt like it was still bubbling away. She loosened her schoolgirl tie for the opening act, breathed deeply and smiled – hoping she wouldn't throw up. Rod had only ever seen her perform once so, on top of not knowing how she felt about him, the fact that he was here was nerve-wracking. Especially as she'd never told him that they were almost naked in the last scene – not that that mattered. She'd told him that it was an aerial show and that she was part of the dance corps. Which was true.

The audience was bigger than usual. Mainly men, as usual, although there was one Portuguese family with two children. She didn't really think it family entertainment but she liked the fact that families came. She spotted Rodrigo out of the corner of her eye. He was sitting on his own at a table, drinking water. He was smiling, his dark eyes focused on her. He was, actually, quite gorgeous. Charlotte had not forgotten of course, but, sitting there in black trousers and a dark shirt, his hair short, black, spiky and shining, he looked particularly stunning. She felt her fixed smile become real and she started to relax and enjoy the performance. It would be all right. Nothing much had happened between her and Ed. She would make sure nothing would ever happen. And, in the meantime, she had this gorgeous man, who was her husband, visiting her. She couldn't wait for the show to end.

After the dancers had taken two bows to the audience, they ran off while the aerialist performers and the two Ivans were taking their bows. Charlotte wiped off her stage make-up, washed and slipped into the casual white pants she had brought with her, a short red top that showed her belly button and a white silk shirt. The other girls wished her luck.

Then she rushed out to meet Rod, who was waiting outside the casino. He kissed her lightly on the lips and didn't even tell her how beautiful she looked. But then he took her hand and guided her down the strip.

'I can't believe you're here. It's such a surprise,' she said.

'Yes, it was for me too.'

'What time did you arrive?'

'About two.'

'Ah Rod. You should have told me.'

'I would have done if I'd known you were going to be out at sea all day but I wanted to surprise you.'

'How long you here for?'

'I'm going back tomorrow.'

'Oh no!' Charlotte couldn't help thinking she was going to be knackered as they had a matinee as well as the evening show on Saturdays.

'I have a match on Sunday.'

He guided her through the palm gardens to one of the posh restaurants on the cliff tops without saying much. She tried to ask him about life in London and Milton Keynes but he just shrugged and said that everything was okay.

'I did think we could have a special dinner so I booked us a table here.'

She didn't like to say that she'd already been here with Ed, twice. 'And what do you think now?' she said, smiling, not sure if he'd confused tenses on purpose or accidentally. He didn't answer. Something was not right. It wasn't so much what he was saying but the spiky gaps in between. Maybe he was missing her and feeling insecure.

'You look gorgeous,' she whispered in his ear. 'I've missed you.'

'Have you?' he said, stopping and looking at her.

'Yes, of course,' she said.

'Do you love me?' he said.

'Of course I love you,' she said. She did. It was just that he had felt so far away, he didn't belong to this part of her life. But now everything would be all right.

The waiter greeted them, particularly her, and showed them to their table where a nice bottle of Esporão wine stood on the table.

'Why you speaking English?' she asked when she heard Rodrigo speaking to the waiter.

He shrugged as they sat down and then spoke Portuguese, only his was different, more melodic and sexy. She gazed at him. He was amazing. He was kind, beautiful, generous, faithful, and when he spoke his native tongue she felt as if fine grains of sand were being sieved over her body. She couldn't wait to take him to the bar to meet her friends. Vicky would love him. Ed would just have to be cool about it. It wasn't like she hadn't warned him.

The waiter spoke English again to tell them the specials, then he left them to study the menu.

'I'm starving,' Charlotte said. 'I think I'll have a steak.'

He looked at her with almost hatred. She blinked in surprise. Where had that come from?

'With all the fresh fish, you want steak?'

'Yes,' Charlotte said. 'I'm fed up of fresh fish. And I've been swimming and dancing all day.'

'Lucky you,' he said, without looking at her.

'Yes,' she said, lighting a cigarette.

He waved his hand in front of himself, as if waving her away. He didn't smoke.

'What's up?' she said. 'I said I was sorry about this afternoon.'

'Nothing. Do you go out often then?'

'Yes, all the time,' Charlotte said. Well, he was winding her up.

'Have you been here before?' he asked.

'Yes,' she said. 'Twice.'

'Who with?'

'Friends.' She paused, angry. 'You don't know them. Yet.'

The waiter appeared and he ordered *sargo* and she steak and chips. Once the waiter had poured the wine, he left them on their own by the open window of the candle-lit banquet hall.

'Cheers,' she said, banging his glass with hers a little too hard. 'It's good to see you.'

He nodded and then said, 'I want you to come home.'

'What?' She looked at him in bewilderment. 'Why.'

'Because I'm not having my wife as a fucking stripper.'

Charlotte felt the red of her shirt rise to her face. 'What?' she said. 'You call taking our tops off in one very short scene when the story demands it stripping?'

'That's what it looked like to me – and every other man there drooling over your bodies.'

'Oh, don't be so fucking twentieth century. Have you walked along the beach?'

'Actually, I have as I didn't have anything else to do this afternoon and most *decent* women were covered.'

'That was here. If you go to other beaches, everyone is topless – at the very least.'

'Well, anyway, a beach is one thing, being topless as a fucking showgirl is another thing entirely. You're like a harem of prostitutes.'

'Oh sweet. Now, you're calling me and my friends prostitutes?' Charlotte wiped out her cigarette. The butt disintegrated.

'What do you expect? Let's be serious, Charlotte. You dance naked, you go out to expensive restaurants with men, you drink all night, you get taken out on boats… and, frankly, fuck knows what else.'

'Oh, don't be so bloody stupid. Yes, we go out but there's nothing going on with anyone. We're just friends having a good time. It's the summer.'

'On whose expense? Someone's paying for your fun, Charlotte. There's no such thing as a free meal and boat ride.'

'Perhaps some people just like our company!'

'No, Charlotte. You either come home…'

'Or? Or what?' she challenged.

'Or we have to rethink. I'm sorry, Charlotte, but you're way out of line. Why didn't you tell me you were going to be a naked showgirl? That's hardly dancing is it? Hardly practising a higher art form. Huh?'

'It's what I enjoy doing, Rodrigo. It's dancing. And if you don't understand that, you can just fuck off.' She stood up. Tears burned her eyes.

'Sit down, Charlotte, you're making a scene.'

'No, I won't sit down and you can fuck off because I'm having the best time of my fucking life.' She turned round, trying to prevent her face from crumbling, and swept past the waiters and the other tables, where bored couples stared at her. Fuck him, really. And fuck them as well.

She practically ran back through the gardens, half afraid he would follow her, half wanting him to, knowing he wouldn't. Miraculously, there was a taxi. She jumped in and asked the driver to take her to the marina. She wiped a rebellious tear and called Ed.

'Charlotte, what's wrong?' His voice was kind, understanding, caring.

'Oh Ed. Rodrigo showed up and we've just had a row. I would love to see you for a minute.'

'Of course, Charlotte. I'll meet you at the marina.'

She put her phone away and felt tears streaming down her face. The taxi driver had the radio on so he couldn't hear her. She wouldn't want anyone to know she was crying. How could he have said those things? Who was he to demand that she give up her job and be a little housey-wife. No way.

Ed was there at the roundabout near the marina. He even paid for the taxi. She hugged him with more passion than she intended.

'Come on,' he said.

'Let's go and talk on the beach,' he said. 'Okay?'

She nodded, wiping her eyes. 'But I'm hungry,' she said.

'Oh really, Charlotte, you should never fight before dinner,' he said in his very American accent.

She smiled.

'I'll go and get a pizza from Pizza Hut and we'll go and sit on the beach. Do you wanna wait here? I'll tell Sarah and Vicky you're here, shall I?'

She nodded and sat down on the wall. Sarah and Vicky came running towards her, arms out, calling her name and she burst into tears again as they hugged her and smothered her in kisses. She told them what had happened. They were silent, except for hushing her, telling her it would be all right, stroking her hair. The only thing Vicky said was: 'You know, Charlotte, you need to decide – in a way, he's made it easier for you. Who are you? Are you the beautiful footballer's wife – who used to be a dancer? Or are you a beautiful dancer who likes to enjoy life, have adventures and meet people?'

'Why can't I be both?' Charlotte asked.

'I guess you have to ask him that.'

Ed returned with pizza and beer and the girls kissed her and told her where they'd be if she needed them.

'Let's go down onto the beach. He may well come looking for you and I don't want to get into a fight with a footballer.' Ed winked at her and she smiled – although she would probably put her money on Ed.

They sat on the beach as she tore through the pizza. She couldn't help thinking of Rodrigo sitting alone in the restaurant. He had come over to see her and she had been out. That must have pissed him off. And she hadn't told him the truth about the show. But then she remembered the way he had looked at her when she ordered a steak. And how he'd called her a prostitute.

'You know, you are going to have to talk this through with him, whatever happens?'

She shrugged.

'Where's he staying?'

'Oriental.'

Ed groaned. 'Great. Maybe he's staying next door. But, really, you should go there. He has come all this way to see you.'

'But he called me a prostitute, Ed. He told me I had to give up doing what I love doing.'

'It's only because he's jealous. He doesn't like the idea of hundreds of men seeing you so sexy. Maybe when he's thought about it, he'll change his mind.'

'You don't mind.'

'What?'

'Hundreds of men seeing me so sexy.'

'No. Jealousy is a bad thing. But I am older and wiser. He is a young, testosterone-filled footballer. He's also probably thinking of the press.'

'But he's not famous!'

'Maybe he will be. He played pretty good the other night.'

'You saw the friendly against Chelsea?'

'Yeah.'

She ate the rest of the pizza and drank her beer without saying anything more. Then she stood up, firmly brushed the sand off her and checked her mobile. There were no missed calls.

'Come on,' she said, holding her hand out to him. 'I want to dance.'

7. The wall

Sonia crossed the road and sat next to Lucinda on the wall opposite the café. She lifted her sunglasses for a moment as she fumbled in her bag for her mobile phone, then glanced casually into the darkness of the bar. The humped-over shadows on the stools didn't resemble Amy or any of her family. Her cousin, Nuno, who worked there, would know where Sonia could find her but, if she went in, her father was sure to hear about it. In this provincial mountain village, she couldn't do anything without him finding out, and he had made it clear that young girls shouldn't be out in bars. Normally, it didn't bother her as the bar was full of stinky old men with dusty hats and no teeth supping *medronho* and tall skinny foreigners with long straggly sand-coloured hair and ripped jeans, Germans mainly. But, today, she wanted to find Amy.

There was no one else on the wall except for Lucinda who was nearly always there at this time of day. Lucinda was waiting for her husband to stumble out. Lucinda couldn't, or wouldn't, go in and she was about fifty years older than Sonia. Sonia looked at her in pity. She would never ever wait for a man to come out of a bar. This must be the most primitive village in Europe, Sonia thought. She couldn't wait to leave.

'Is he still in there then, Dona Lucinda?' she said.

Lucinda nodded and didn't reply.

Two days ago Sonia had been walking past the bus stop after school when an English girl had stopped to ask her when the next bus to Monchique was. Sonia had told her it was in two hours' time and then they sat together and began talking. Amy understood Portuguese but preferred to speak English which suited Sonia fine as Sonia needed to practise English so that one day she could escape. Amy was two years younger than her, fifteen, although she looked older. She was dark, like Sonia, and she had moved to Boa Vista, just outside of Monchique, six months ago in the middle of

January. There were a few Boa Vistas around and Sonia wasn't sure which one it was.

'It's in the middle of nowhere,' Amy said.

'How do you get there from Monchique?'

'I have to walk half a day.'

'Bad luck.'

'Yeah, but I'm not staying in there.' She pointed to the café. 'We came to play pool but they're all drunk.'

'Who?'

'All of them. My mum, my nan, her partner, her ex-boyfriend, Rich, and Bill, he's one of nan's mates who's a builder, and some other friends. Marcus, he's a muso. You know, after one drink, they relax, after two drinks they're all smiles, after three drinks they'll give you extra pocket money. After four they'll want you to buy *them* a drink. And after five, they stand on their heads, or do the splits, or something *really* embarrassing.'

'Oh.' Sonia had no idea what the splits were but she understood that Amy's entire family were drunk. In Sonia's family, only her dad and brother drank – and rarely at home.

'I wish I could drive. There's our car.' Amy tossed her head back towards where a Mercedes, an old Renault and a red VW were parked. Sonia wasn't sure which one she meant.

'So you all live here?'

'Yeah, pretty much. My nan moved out here first, then everyone kind of followed. They'd all had enough of England. Nan was a psychology lecturer at the university for thirty-two years so she knows a lot of people.'

'Who is "Nan"?' Sonia asked.

'Nan, you know, gran, grandmother.'

'Your grand*mother* was a psychology lecturer?' Sonia didn't know that grandmothers could be lecturers.

'Yes. What's so strange?'

'Nothing. Why did she move here?'

'Dunno. The weather's crap, of course, in England. It's very expensive. And my nan says that the people are like rats in a cage.'

Sonia couldn't imagine England as an expensive cage. Everyone knew it was a rich civilised country where people lived in big houses, were polite to each other and drove big cars. Not like most of the people in the village who still lived in shacks without bathrooms, shouted at each other and drove donkeys. Her father had an Audi though.

'Are you going to school?' Sonia asked.

'Yeah, Monchique, but we're off now of course for the summer.'

'How is it?'

'It's okay. The teachers are kind. But it's hard to make friends. Luckily, there are a few other international students.'

Sonia wanted to give Amy her mobile number but the bus from Monchique came and her aunt got off it. She must have been visiting her sister.'

'Sonia, what luck you are here, *menina*,' her aunt said, laden with Alisuper shopping bags.

'Yes, I'm just with a friend, *Tia*,' Sonia explained before turning to Amy. 'I'm sorry but I have to go.' She would have to help her aunt.

'No worries,' Amy said. 'Come and visit sometime. Nuno knows where we live. You know the guy behind the bar in the café.'

'Yeah, okay,' Sonia replied.

Later that evening, her father had asked her, 'So what were you doing at the bus-stop today?' His moustache was twitching. There was just her and her mother, her brother was out – in a bar. They were sitting in the dining room with the window open but the blinds down. Her mother was dishing up 'bacalhau à brás'. *O Preco Certo* blasted out from several TVs. The short brash presenter surrounded by plastic women with moulded hairstyles and painted smiles made Sonia want to scream. She would much rather watch *Morangos com Açúcar* but her father didn't approve. It showed girls of her age in bars and restaurants enjoying themselves.

'I met an English girl who is living here. She is happy for me to practise English.'

'Who is she?'

'Her name is Amy.'

'Amy? Her mother was in the café today,' her father said. 'She is a drunk.'

Sonia paused. She could feel her cheeks flushing.

'That doesn't mean to say that she's a bad person,' she said.

'Women who drink are either whores or mad,' her father said.

'What about men who drink?' Sonia said.

'What about men who drink?' her father asked, picking up his fork. 'They're men, aren't they. Of course, they drink. What do you expect? They have to go out to work all day, provide for their families, put up with you lot. Of course they drink.'

'So what about the women who have to look after men. And have to work? Don't you think they deserve to drink?'

There was a silence. Her mother touched her father's arm.

'Go to your room. NOW.'

'Oi *querido*, don't let's make a scene. I'm sure she's not going to have anything to do with the family, are you Sonia?'

'No, *Mãe*.' Sonia got up.

'Go to your room and stay there. Think about how disrespectful you were,' her father said, food spilling out of his mouth.

Sonia left the room, calmly, even though she felt as if her heart would explode. She got to her bedroom and switched on her laptop, reminding herself that she had only one more year left and then she was going to university. Coimbra would be the best as it was further away but Évora would also be fine. Faro was too close. She hadn't told her parents yet. She either wanted to study psychology or law. She decided then that she wanted to speak to Amy's grandmother. She would need to start applying soon.

Later, she apologised to her father. He was watching the news about the little girl who'd disappeared. Her parents were standing outside the church in Luz. There was still no sign of the little girl. 'Look at her,' her father said. 'Such a beautiful woman.' She was clearly not a whore then, Sonia thought. Even though it was said she'd left the three children alone in a room while she was out drinking. Sonia bit her tongue. At that particular moment a year seemed like eternity.

Sonia got up when Lucinda's husband finally zig-zagged out, waving behind at his shadowy mates stuck to the bar stools.

'Oh, there you are, woman,' he called to Lucinda. 'I's just having a little drink before dinner.'

Lucinda held onto him as he staggered beside her. Sonia shook her head in pity and disgust. She needed to find Amy. Maybe she should take the bus to Monchique.

An old Mercedes pulled up and a man with dark grey hair and glasses got out. Behind his glasses shone blue eyes. Before she had time to think twice, Sonia walked towards the car.

'Excuse me?' she said. He looked at her in surprise. 'Do you know Amy?'

The man smiled. 'Yes, I'm part of her family.'

'Can you give her my number? We met two days ago.'

'I can take you to see her if you want? If you wait here a sec. I just want to speak to Nuno in the café about something.'

'Okay, but can we meet by the bus-stop?' Sonia did not want Nuno to see her getting into the man's car.

'Sure.'

Sonia hoped she wasn't making a mistake as she yanked open the Mercedes' door and got in. She knew it wasn't a good idea to get into strange men's cars. Flashes of empty roads and dark, windy nights made her clutch her mobile a little tighter as they bumped the last speed bump out of the village and hit the open road, flanked on both sides by eucalyptus and cork oak. But he had a nice smile. His name was Rich.

'How long have you been here?' she asked him.

'We moved here last July – a year ago. And you? Were you born here?'

'Yes,' she said.

'It's quite unusual to meet young Portuguese ladies here,' Rich said. 'Do your parents lock you all up?' He turned and smiled at her.

'Yes,' she said, smiling back.

'I did wonder,' he said.

'We have to help with the family, the cooking, that sort of thing. It's not usual for women to go out to the bars.'

'Well, you're probably not missing much. But that's not really the point, is it?' he said, as if to himself.

'I think the people are backward here in the mountains. I want to go to university.'

'Good for you. What are you going to study?'

'I'm not sure yet. Either psychology or law.'

'I'm a psychology graduate. A post-graduate actually.'

'Really?' Her heart pounded. 'And what do you work?'

'I'm not working now but I worked for the council in England. You know the *Câmara*?' She nodded, failing to see the connection between the council and psychology. 'I used to section people.'

'What does that mean?'

'You know when someone with mental problems is unable to take care of themselves, we step in and take control and make them go into hospital or care.'

'The council do that?'

'Yes, don't they here?'

'I don't think so. I think that would be up to the family.'

94

At least, she hoped it would. If her father had that power he would go around and arrest all women in bars.

'Look at that view,' he said as the south coast glittered down below them to the right. 'It's very beautiful. You are lucky to be born here.'

Sonia said 'yes' but didn't agree. She sunk into the leather seat on spotting her cousin, Zé, debarking eucalyptus poles at the side of the road. She didn't think he had seen her.

They turned off towards Chilrão, Pe do Frio and Selão. The road curved up until they were parallel with the west coast. She hadn't been along this road for years – there was no bus service this way. Sonia had thought they lived the other side of Monchique but Rich explained that they could either go via Monchique or this way. She began to worry about getting back. She wouldn't be allowed out for a month if her father found out. She looked at her watch – it was nearly five o'clock.

'Don't worry, I can take you back later.'

'Thank you.'

They passed one of the five wind turbines staggered up the mountain, the gleaming white blades idling in circles against the late afternoon blue sky. Sonia had recently read Don Quixote and could easily imagine some of the people from her village riding on donkeys up to the turbines and waving their fists at them. Or, more likely, offering them shots of *medronho*.

'I know some people who live near here and they say that it is like living near an airport. We don't hear them, do you?' the man asked.

'Sometimes, on a quiet day, but not very much. We are ten kilometres away.' Her father had told her that there had been a few complaints to the President. Her father sympathised – he wouldn't like to live near them – but everyone else in the Council was proud of their renewable energy. Buy earplugs had been the answer.

They were almost at Monchique when Rich pulled off the road and down a drive, parking at the bottom. There were four small stone houses that she could see staggered into the hill below the road facing the west coast. Hazy blue light blurred the edges of the mountains as they folded away in front of her, smaller and smaller until they reached the sea. Sonia couldn't help gazing at the view.

'The land's only just recovering after the fires,' Rich said.

'Did it burn here?'

'Yep. I wasn't here. But everyone else had to evacuate.'

95

She didn't say she knew some of the local kids who had started at least one of the fires.

'Amy?' Rich called as they went down the path towards the stone houses. 'A friend to see you.'

Amy came out of the last house chewing something. She looked surprised to see her.

'Hi. I'm just having my tea. Would you like some?'

Thinking it would be rude to say no, Sonia agreed, and they all went in. She was greeted by a large space with a spiral staircase in the middle going up to another room. On the walls were large modern paintings and wall lights made out of roof tiles with holes cut in them. At a quick glance, Sonia counted five people and one little boy of about four, as well as Amy and herself. They were all speaking English, including the plasma television on the wall. A tall woman with long blonde straight hair and hazel eyes, wearing a long flared purple skirt, flat sandals and a white cotton blouse with sequins and buttons up to the neck, was cooking. Rich introduced Sonia as 'Amy's friend' and then went to help the tall woman with the food. There were shouts of 'Welcome Amy's friend'. Sonia smiled at everyone.

An old woman with feathery white hair, a tanned face with more lines than bark in a tree and piercing black eyes sat at an enormous wooden table. She must be the grandmother, Amy thought. Another man with deep gullies in his face, wearing a dusty hat and a handkerchief around his neck, sat next to her. Two small dogs meandered hopefully around the tall blonde woman and Rich, who were carrying steaming saucepans. In one corner of the room there was a small stage with a set of drums, a guitar and a computer. A white cat slept on a large leather sofa in front of the television. Sonia felt as if she had been beamed onto Mars. There was no table cloth, or serviettes, or photographs of the family smiling down from laced-over sideboards. There were no statues of any of the saints or any religious symbols, and there was no china or trinkets decorating the room.

'Sit down, sit down, Amy's friend,' the tall woman told her. 'Would you like some bangers and mash?'

Sonia hesitated. She had absolutely no idea what the woman meant but she didn't think it was a type of tea.

'Mum, she won't know what that is. It's mashed potato and sausage.'

'Oh, okay, thank you,' Sonia said. She stared at Amy's mother: she didn't look like a drunk, or a prostitute. She wasn't even wearing make-up.

A plate each of mashed potato, orange beans and two short, fat sausages fell in front of her and Amy.

The grandmother sat at the head of the table. 'So what is your name, Amy's friend?' she asked her. Her small eyes scanned her like a photocopier.

'Sonia,' she said.

'We met outside the café the other day when you were all getting drunk,' Amy added.

'Getting drunk? I don't remember getting drunk. Do you?' The grandmother looked around at the other people in the kitchen who all shook their heads.

Sonia tried to imagine having this kind of conversation with her grandmother.

'Sonia wants to be a psychologist,' Rich said, picking up a fork.

'So why do you want to study psychology, Sonia?' the grandmother asked.

'Well, I'm not sure if I want to study psychology or law,' Sonia said, trying some of the potato. It was good. Feeling braver, she tried cutting a sausage.

'Law is easier to spell,' the old woman said seriously.

Sonia smiled.

'Nan, stop it. Anyway, you don't know anything about Portuguese law.'

'Only that the law is one thing, society is another. Isn't that right, Sonia?' The grandmother winked at her.

Sonia nodded, trying the sausage. She was right. Look at the way old Lucinda waited on the wall. It was wrong that women should wait on walls for men. Sonia's teeth cracked the sausage skin and gristles of fat exploded into her mouth.

'Sonia, I have counselled people all my life and they're still fucked up. On the other hand, the Law is an ass, as Mr Bumble says, – and needs changing.'

'Ah, don't you ever shut the fuck up,' the one with the hat muttered.

'No, no, this young Portuguese lady has come to see me. She wants to ask my advice. Isn't that right, Sonia?'

She nodded, wondering how the grandmother could possibly have known, and who Mr Bumble was.

'That's all right, they don't understand,' the grandmother continued. 'You want to do something with your life and change the world you live in, don't you? Only now you're not sure how you are going to go about it.'

Sonia nodded, shuffling some orange beans into her mouth so she wouldn't have to speak. They were sweet.

'Let me ask you, why would you want to study psychology?'

Sonia swallowed. 'I'm interested in people and, erm, how they think.'

'Okay, that's a good reason. And, now tell me, why would you want to study law?'

'Because I'm interested in human rights. I think many women don't know their rights. I would like to help them.'

'Then, Sonia, I think you have answered your own question.'

'Leave the girl alone, Mum, and eat your tea,' Amy's mum said.

They all became silent as they ate. Sonia scooped up the last of the now orange potato and rested her knife and fork together on the plate.

'Come on, Sonia. Have you finished? Let me show you the tree house.'

The grandmother winked at her when they left. Sonia smiled back and thanked them all. Rich said he would take her home whenever she wanted. Sonia had never met such kind people.

Amy took her down a path crossing several terraces. There were fruit trees and flowers but no sign of agriculture. In one of the cork oaks they had built a small wooden house. There was a short ladder going up to it. Sonia followed Amy, crawling through a small wooden door into the room with a glass window facing out to the mountains and the west coast. The view was framed in the little window making it look like a water painting.

'What a cool place, Amy. And what an amazing family. You are so lucky.'

Amy snorted. 'They're all nuts.'

'Maybe, but they are so...' Sonia struggled to find the words. 'Free, I guess.'

'Well, Nan always insists on us all being ourselves. She says we can never be happy if we are trying to be someone we're not.'

Sonia thought about her mother. She had never been allowed to be herself and she wasn't happy. She defined herself by the roles she played as both mother and obedient housewife who shopped,

cooked, cleaned and looked after them. Her parents, Sonia's grandparents, had worked the land but her mother had married a richer man so she didn't have to grow potatoes. She often said she wished she had a plot of land to cultivate. Maybe that's who she really was? Her father was allowed to be himself and he still wasn't happy. But maybe that was because their society didn't allow him to be himself. Or maybe he didn't know himself who he was. Sonia wasn't sure. But she knew that she was going to be herself: she would never wait on a wall outside a café and that she was going to Coimbra to study law – and find out why Mr Bumble called it an ass.

8. Azar

'Fucking shit, we need money, you asshole.'

João became conscious of Sasha standing above him, arms folded, chewing like a cow. He burst out laughing, a high-pitched snigger. Staring up at her black eyes and white face, she looked a bit like a cow.

'What now? I think you not understand we have *no-thing*...' She sliced her arm through the air, '...to eat. Or drink. Or smoke.'

'Don't make problems, Sasha. I am rich soon. If not, then we go to Portimão and you can do some business,' João said, still sniggering. He wished he had a daisy to put in her mouth.

'We are dead before you rich. And you have no car. How we get to Portimão without car? Hm? Answer me. Clever ass. You think I go on bus? You need to think again, Mister Jowow.'

She kicked him. He turned over, his body convulsed with laughter.

'You think I funny? Let me tell you, Mister Jowow, I am out of here when I have money. You think I need you? You think I need this shit?'

João's body shuddered to a halt and he turned back to face her.

'Ah Sashinha, my little sweet angel, don't worry. Mister Jowow arrange something. Now, just get me a coffee and brandy and I think.' João half sat up on the mattress on the floor. He was naked except for the kaffiyeh hanging from his head. He straightened it.

'No coffee. No brandy. No cigarette. No dope. No drug. No food. No clothes. No nothing. You think I am used to live like this in Russia? Huh? In Russia we have all these things.'

'Ah Sashinha, we have beautiful house in beautiful village in beautiful Algarve. This is Salema where all the rich and famous buy houses.'

'But you not rich and famous. You beggar. Your house fall down. You have no places to sit or eat. And this is shitty fishing village with no place to make money.'

'Then we go to Russia,' João said, the smirk fading from his face as he slowly woke up.

'No, you cretin. *I* go to Russia. You stay in shitty fishing village.'

João was constantly amazed at her vocabulary in English. What did 'cretin' mean? He was going to ask her but she was walking away from him. 'Sasha! Come back. You miss the boat if you go now.' But she'd already gone.

João rummaged around for his shorts on the floor next to him and took out his wallet. He was sure he had borrowed ten euros from Jorge last night, but it wasn't there. She'd probably stolen it. He switched his mobile on. It was three o'clock. He had a missed call from Ahmad. This was it! The boat was ready! Sasha had no patience. His hands shook and he could feel his stomach rotting on the inside. But now wasn't the time to think of his deteriorating body as he needed a pen. He got and walked naked throughout all three storeys of the dark shuttered house. 'Where the fuck has she hidden all the pens?' he shouted.

'You talk about me?' she said, appearing at the door with two coffees and a not quite empty bottle of *Macieira*.

'Sashinha, angel, let me help you.' He took the bottle of brandy from her, opened the top and took a large gulp. He shivered. 'I was looking for a pen.'

'A pen? Why you need pen? You not write.'

'I need to write down coordinates for pick-up.'

'What pick-up? You pick-up more girls? I tell them that you are big shit.'

'No, for merchandise, Sasha. Merchandise. To sell. To make money.'

'Oh, okay, then I have pen.'

She opened her bag on her shoulder and pulled out a blue biro.

'And paper?'

'You are very difficult man.' She tore up a tampon box. 'Here.'

'You are the best, Sasha.'

'I know. But still you treat me like piece of shit.'

João drank some more brandy, knocked back the *bica* and then called Ahmad.

'Hey Ahmad, friend, where do I go?'

João listened carefully, his head beginning to throb as he translated Ahmad's coded instructions. The drop-off would be at 2 a.m. tomorrow. João repeated the coordinates which Ahmad gave him as a phone number. If there were waves of more than one metre, force four, they would abort. But there wouldn't be – it was August. João would abort if a wave so much as rocked the boat but he wasn't the one going out. Then João was to sell the shit and they would split the profits. Perfect. Twenty kilos. Ten thousand euros. He had promised to pay his cousin, Pedro, two thousand for doing the run.

'Well?' Sasha said, nailing him with her dirty black eyes.

'You are looking at rich man, Sasha.' He jumped up and held out his hand. She slapped him but he managed to get her to stand up and they waltzed around the dark room before collapsing on the one piece of furniture other than the mattress – the table.

'You see my beautiful Russian princess, I will buy you everything.'

'You buy me ticket back to beautiful Russia?'

'Anything, you want.' He started massaging her neck until she began to relax. Then he kissed her – hundreds of little kisses all over her neck and shoulders. He could feel her melting like an ice cube in his mouth. She let him slip a hand beneath her T-shirt and he unhooked her bra so he could feel her breasts. She lay on the table as he kissed her belly button. She was beginning to purr which meant that it was usually safe to have sex at this stage. But João was never too sure so he held her arms down as he shuffled on top of the table.

'You are the best, Sasha,' he whispered, kissing her on the mouth so she couldn't say anything.

'So where is money?' she asked, as she rearranged her bra.

'On the boat.'

'Where is boat?' She drank the rest of the *Macieira*.

'Morocco.' He got off the table and walked around the room to find his clothes.

'Morocco, you monkey ass. You think I go to that stinking country to get your money?'

'No, Sashinha, the hash is on the boat that we meet tonight. Ahmad know the captain of big fishing boat and he go to Espanha and Portugal to drop off to smaller boats two kilometres from coast.'

'Now you want me to be fishing woman and catch drugs in Atlantico?'

'No, Sasha, Pedro go out and meet them.' Pedro had the fastest boat in the Algarve.

'He too drunk.'

'He'll be fine.'

'He know that it tonight?'

'Not yet.'

'Then call him, asshole.'

João thought about hitting her but she had moved away. Instead, he called Pedro and asked if he could take them shopping that evening. This was the code word. Pedro didn't sound too happy, saying that he had beautiful dancers to entertain. João told him to bring them over and he would entertain them.

'Entertain who?' Sasha sniped.

'Shut up Sasha,' he said. 'This is important.'

Pedro said he would come over and they would talk. Ten minutes later, he walked in with a beer in his hand.

'Hey João. Did you know it's August and summer out there?'

'Hey cousin, any beer for us?'

Pedro pulled out another bottle of Cristal from his pocket.

'Here, split that.'

João opened the bottle with his teeth and took a long gulp. He would have drunk it all but Sasha snatched the bottle from him.

'You must think more. Not drink more.'

Pedro laughed which annoyed João.

'So, are you in?' João asked harshly.

'High tide is 6 a.m. and you want me to meet the boat at 2 a.m.? Let me see the coordinates.'

João showed him.

'That's just off the coast here,' Pedro said.

'Yes, very easy. Ahmad says that it is force two or, at most, force three.'

'Except my boat is in Lagos.'

'Oh.' João hadn't thought of that when he had told Ahmad that the drop off was to be in Salema.

'It's not a problem but I have to get back to Lagos as I need it there tomorrow. Besides, if Jorge and the fishermen see me in the village they will know something's up.'

'Then we wait for you on beach. You drop it to us at end of beach. And you go,' Sasha said. 'Simple.'

João looked at Pedro. She was right as usual.

'What about tourists?' Pedro asked. 'It's peak season.'

'We make sure no tourists,' Sasha said, taking charge. João didn't like it when she did that.

'Who is we?' Pedro asked.

'Me and him.' She pointed a bony finger at João.

'He needs to come with me,' Pedro said. 'I'm not going out on my own. So that means you need to pick the shit up from the beach.'

'I'm not picking up your shit.'

João lit a cigarette. Things were not going to plan. João had no intention of going on any boat, any more than he had of Sasha organising his life.

'I will wait on the beach with Sasha,' João said. 'You don't need me.'

'I do need you.'

João pulled hard on the cigarette. This was becoming tricky.

'Why don't you take Jowow with you and drop all shit in Salema? Then you go back to Lagos on your own?' Sasha said.

'Maybe but it would be better if there were two of us,' Pedro said thoughtfully. 'It is dangerous for one man on his own at night and there are still many more police boats out at sea because of that missing girl.'

'If many police, better Jowow not with you.'

'Maybe. What if boat is not there?' Pedro asked João.'

João sighed smoke. 'It will be. He says only to abort if more than force five.'

'You still pay me if we abort?'

João shrugged, ignoring Sasha's snorting. He meant to ask about the missing girl but Sasha was pawing at the table.

'And you pay me also?' she asked, tapping her red chipped nails. 'Or maybe I don't wait on beach.'

'I pay you twenty,' João said.

'Then I don't wait.'

'Thirty.'

'Two hundred.'

'Ah Sasha. I pay everything for you. Fifty – final offer.'

She thought for a minute and then scowled an upside down smile and said, 'Hm'.

'If we abort I send you text – *No fish in sea*. Okay?'

'How you send text? You no credit.'

João considered strangling her.

'You have no money, cousin?' Pedro asked.

'He has *no-thing*.'

'Shut up. Once we get the shit, I will have.'

'Let me buy you two a brandy. And we'll put some credit on your phone. Then we go.' Pedro got off the table and headed towards the door. Sasha followed him, grabbing her floppy purple hat while João swapped his kaffiyeh for his straw hat and slipped his feet into well-worn flip-flops. 'It's almost five,' Pedro continued, lighting a cigarette. 'And, thanks to you, I need to cancel my date with the most beautiful woman in the world.'

'Who is she?' João asked, squinting his eyes against the golden day as they went down the steps to the cobbled road. He could feel the sweat dripping from his straw hat almost immediately. For some strange reason, women found Pedro attractive. He had so many girlfriends and three kids from different women. Not that João could talk: he had two kids. Sasha promised him she didn't want children but women always said that until they turned thirty and then – bang – he was up shit creek. Well, they were up shit creek. But, he had to admit, Sasha was different.

'She is a dancer in the show at the casino in Portimão. English, tall, blonde, sexy, late twenties.'

João laughed. 'Another *bife*.'

'No, really, she is special.'

'She prostitute,' Sasha said, rummaging in her bag. She produced her purple-lensed sunglasses and put them on.

'No, I don't think so,' Pedro said.

'She's not like you,' João said and braced himself as she dug her nails into his arm.

'Of course, she is, stupid man. She showgirl. In Russia all showgirls prostitutes.'

Pedro shrugged as if to say he didn't care if she was. João made a mental note that he and Pedro should go to see the show.

The village square was packed with cars, and tourists carrying beach mats, umbrellas, bucket and spades, towels and various other objects necessary for an afternoon on the beach. João sniggered at them all, particularly the families, like a herd of sheep. The beach café heaved with the slightly undercooked flesh, pinkened and softened by the grilling sun, sweat trickling down their faces.

They sat outside the *pastelaria* in the shade and Pedro went to get them coffee, brandies and *bifanas* after Sasha said that she would not go the beach unless she ate a pork sandwich.

Jorge and little Mário sat at a table near him. Jorge was drinking beer and Mário sat, silently clutching a 7-Up bottle. It had been a black day in the village when his father had drowned at sea. The same thing had happened to João's grandfather – most of the village knew someone from their family who'd been lost at sea, but it shouldn't happen these days – boats were safer.

'Pedro – your boat is unsinkable, right?' he asked as he came back carrying a tray of drinks.

'Of course. It is a semi-rigid.'

'Why? You scared to die? It would be big happiness.'

'Don't give up hope, Sasha,' Pedro said seriously. 'It can still tip up.'

João felt momentarily weak. The sea was an immense flooded graveyard as far as he was concerned and to be avoided at all costs. Unfortunately, he couldn't get out of this one and he didn't want Pedro to know how afraid he was of the sea so he didn't say anything. Antonio, the owner of the *pastelaria*, brought them the *bifanas*. Sasha whipped hers off the plate.

'What does "tipup" mean?' she asked, her mouth snapping at the *bifana*.

'Turn over.' Pedro illustrated with his hands what he meant.

'Oh good.' She munched.

'If I died, you wouldn't have anything,' João said moodily, imagining himself sinking into the water, a line of bubbles being his only link with the world he'd known.

'*Bozhe moi!...*'

She began shouting at him in Russian. João ignored her and started talking to Pedro about his boat. Zé, who worked at the restaurant Paraíso, came by in a white apron and shook hands with João and Pedro and kissed Sasha – which, at least, shut her up.

'He is nice man,' she said, after he'd gone to talk to Jorge.

Everyone knew Zé was a bad boy who drank too much, shagged too many tourists and gambled.

'Too nice for you, Sasha.'

'We see.'

João laughed at the thought of Sasha with Zé. Sasha was youngish and still attractive, when she wasn't chewing like a cow with mascara smudged around her eyes, but no one else would put up with her craziness. Except for maybe Zé. He stopped laughing.

'A beer?' Pedro asked.

João nodded.

'No, I think it better you go.'

'Ah Sasha, you are becoming a nag.'

'I'm not nag. I need money, asshead.'

João sniggered and lent over to kiss her. Her butchery of the English language was very sexy. Pedro, also laughing, stood up to get some beer, prising open his mobile as if opening a clam.

'Even he have money,' Sasha said, wiping a stray onion with a dirty finger and shovelling it into her mouth.

'Then go live with him,' João said, slinging his right leg over his left thigh and putting his hands behind his head, relaxing with the thought of not having her nagging him any more.

Pedro was still talking on his mobile when he came back with three bottles of Cristal. 'So, we make tomorrow, okay? Enjoy the show... You not going? ... Three times?' He put the beers on the table. João noticed Pedro's hands were still shaking despite the brandies. His were feeling good now. Sasha never seemed to shake – Russians must be born with a super alcohol tolerance. Pedro snapped the phone shut.

'You talk to pimp?' Sasha asked, before stopping her mouth with the bottle.

Pedro laughed. 'Kind of. This American guy, Ed, loads of dough. Paid me three hundred euros to take them out on the boat a couple of weeks ago. Him and three dancers. And provided champagne.'

'You give me number?' Sasha said, wiping a tear of beer from her chin. 'Shit.'

'I'll bring him here one day and you can meet him.'

'Thank God.'

'You don't believe in God, Sasha,' João said.

'Now I do.'

'Okay, are you ready?' Pedro sucked out the remaining beer from the bottle.

João did the same and lent over to kiss Sasha goodbye. She didn't kiss him back but she didn't move away so that was okay. She was fiddling with the label on the bottle as if planning something. Zé was still there talking with Jorge. Oh, what the hell. If she wanted to shag him that was up to her. She waved at him as they got in Pedro's old diesel Mercedes. João's last car had been a Renault 4 but he'd had to use it to pay for the drinks one night at the bad luck bar, the Azar, when Rui had refused to serve him any more until he paid for the last six months. Very unreasonable. But he'd since learned that the car had refused to start. *Azar.*

They drove to Lagos, the sun behind them. Pedro talked about this showgirl, Vicky, all the way. She had him by the balls. João would never let that happen. Men and women weren't designed to be together for long so it wasn't worth getting too involved. They had different cycles: sometimes they would find themselves on the same path at the same time and they rolled along in unison. But then one of them would hit a rock and they would change direction. That it was time to part. Either that or he would run out of money and they would mysteriously disappear.

Pedro parked up next to a red Porsche near the marina in front of the old railway station. João remembered first coming here as a little boy when they had gone to visit an old aunt in Portimão. It wasn't that long ago and yet it had been another world. The station had been surrounded by donkeys and carts, old women in headscarves or hats and long, full skirts, carrying endless bundles. The café had been full of smoky men in patched up dark jackets, leather boots, trilby hats and drinking beer. He remembered staring at the boots as he didn't have any. He burst out laughing when he realised he still didn't have any. Pedro laughed with him as if sharing the joke but João thought he was just pissed.

They got to the boat, after buying some beer. It looked like a big dinghy, João thought, still laughing, before deciding it wasn't funny. The boat was called 'Storm' – a stupid name for a boat.

It roared to life. João tried very hard not to trip over the ropes as he threw them in and stepped over the black rubber rim into the boat. Pedro expertly reversed away from the pontoon, under the bridge and stopped to fill up with diesel. He also filled a spare canister – just in case.

'No one will think it strange if we go out now,' Pedro said, starting the engine.

Most boats were coming in, although there were a few small motor boats heading out to see the sunset. João paid for the fuel and then they set out along the Rio towards the sea. It was a hot July evening and people strolled along the Avenida, faces glowing like setting suns, dressed up to go to the restaurants. No one paid them any attention.

Pedro chugged slowly towards the horizon and they watched the bruised sky bleed into the sea. João couldn't remember the last time he had seen a sunset. Sasha wasn't interested in stuff like that. Then Pedro headed east – just in case anyone was tracking them. At Carvoeiro, Pedro cut the engine. Then they cracked open a beer and smoked a joint that Pedro had brought with him. As João sat there, bobbing up and down, he felt a calmness he had not felt for a long time. Maybe a life at sea wasn't so bad after all.

Problems began around midnight. They'd drunk all the alcohol and João had been dozing but then the sea kicked up and his stomach began to feel queasy. Pedro was silent and, on investigation, João discovered that he was fast asleep, his hand moving with the wheel. He shook him and Pedro opened glassy eyes, looking at João as if he were a ghost. A wave splashed over the side of the boat.

'Fucking hell, Pedro. We were asleep. Now where are we?'

Pedro shook himself, hacked and spat at the sea. He checked the coordinates.

'Bollocks,' he said. 'Have we any brandy?'

'No,' João growled, his belly now tumbling like a washing machine rinsing on beer and brandy. Surely he couldn't be seasick. He came from centuries of fishermen.

'Bollocks,' Pedro growled, another big wave breaking onto the boat.

'Do you have to do that?' João said.

'I can't control the waves, cousin.'

'Should we abort? The sea is getting rougher.'

Pedro laughed. 'This is nothing.'

He guided the boat through the waves, hitting every one he possibly could. João sat still holding on. He didn't know if he could move as his legs felt somehow disconnected. He stared up at the roof of stars but they kept jumping up and down as they went over the waves. The same thing happened with the distant pin-prick lights on the coast. He didn't know if he could hold on for much longer.

'Where are we?'

'Near Cavoeiro.'

João sniggered and then, when he realised Pedro was not joking, that they had drifted the wrong way, he turned and hung over the rounded rubber side of the boat and vomited.

'Shitting hell, João, what's going on?'

João groaned but couldn't respond. He felt weaker than he'd ever felt and the thought of another hour on this vomit bowl made him want to throw himself overboard and drown. Only the thought of Sasha's joyous face looming over his corpse saved him.

'Don't lie down, you'll feel worse.'

But he couldn't stand up. And he was struggling to sit up. He felt himself slide down the wet rubber and onto the wet floor. But he didn't care. He just wanted to get off this boat. Until then he couldn't move.

'Fuck, João, you could have told me you got seasick.' Pedro cursed noisily as the boat smashed through the dark waves. João listened but felt his brain closing down as he imagined himself in the Azar, listening to 'Rock the Kasbah', desperately trying to block out the noise of the boat's engine and the waves breaking and crashing around the boat. Hours seem to pass, tipping up and down, side to side.

'That must be it,' he heard Pedro say. 'João, get up! Asshole! There she is! I'm gonna flash the spotlight three times.'

João tried to move but the boat tipped.

'Okay, now all we need do is find the package.' Pedro circled round over the waves while João continued to rock around the floor of the boat. 'There it is! João! There it is!' Pedro changed direction and then put the engine into neutral while he leant over the side and fished out a five-litre water bottle with three luminous thick balloons around it. He threw it at João.

'There, make a joint.'

João propped himself up in time to see a large shadow creep slowly away into the darkness.

'Okay, now we head for the beach and let's hope there's no cops. Or tourists. Then you can get off as you're as much help as a dead fish.'

João lapped up those words like ice-cream. He would be off the vomit bowl soon. And he would be with Sasha. And he had the booty. He almost felt better but then João revved up the boat and they began to jump the waves at about thirty knots. He fell back down onto the wet rubber.

Pedro chugged towards the beach. It was calmer nearer the coast and João felt life glide back into his body. Several night fishing boats dotted the sea, like fallen stars. Street lights on the promenade and car park by the beach lit up the dark metallic hulks of cars, silent. Only the sound of music and laughter came from the Azar. It must be about 2 a.m., closing time.

'Okay, João, you ready? I think the beach is clear.'

João lifted himself up and grabbed the bottle. He tried to take the balloons off but Pedro insisted that he take them with him. João

110

wasn't in a position to argue. He sat back up on the seat for the first time in hours. 'Fucking hell, never again,' he said.

'Too right, cousin.'

Pedro took him to the shore at the side of the beach and João climbed gratefully into the sea. The tide was out as predicted so he was still a way from the village. He thought he saw a few shadows on the beach but no Sasha.

'Where is the cow?' he muttered. 'Will you be okay?' he asked Pedro.

'Better than you.'

Pedro turned the boat and headed back out to sea. João fell onto the sand, the bottle and balloons next to him. He needed to rest after the worst night of his life. He would never ever get into a boat again. He lay down on the wet sand and called Sasha on his mobile but she didn't answer.

Fifteen minutes later, she still hadn't shown up and João began to shiver. But at least he could stand. He needed to get rid of the balloons so he untied them, tried to puncture them and threw them out to sea. But they glowed like fluorescent footballs. He retrieved them and began to pile them under some stones. Maybe she had fallen asleep? He tried calling her again but nothing. He remembered that he didn't have a key to the house. 'Fucking bitch,' he muttered. He would put her straight back onto a flight to beautiful Russia. He picked up the five-litre bottle of hash packed with foam. The GNR often lurked in the village at night so he didn't particularly want to walk around with it. He took some out and then buried the bottle higher up on the rocks where the tide wouldn't reach it. Then he brushed himself down and headed to the village. There was no sign of anyone, all the bars were shut and no one was in his house. 'Shit, shit, shit.' He called Sasha again. This time she answered. He could hear music and drinking in the background.

'Where the fuck are you?' he hissed.

'Oh Mr Jowow. I at fucking awesome party. I make drinks. They pay me one hundred euros.'

Words flew from his mouth but were captured by the dark and left him gagging.

'You have nice boat trip?'

'Sasha, I am cold, I am standing outside my house and can not get in. Will you fucking come here and let me in?'

'No. I work until six.'

'Where are you?'

'Big villa on top of hill.'

'What's it called,' João said, grinding his teeth. He would kill her when he found her.

'I not tell you. You make big drama.'

'Tell me, Sashinha. Jowow needs to sleep.'

'No.' She cut the phone off.

João felt the scream form in the pit of his stomach and gather strength as it passed his lungs and up through his larynx. He opened his mouth to let it out but put his fist in just in time to stop it: the whole village would hear him. Instead he climbed his own steps and lay down outside his door.

Next thing he knew a blinding light whipped at his eyes and something was kicking him in the back.

'Jowow, wake up!'

He blinked at Sasha's legs standing above him wearing a short red skirt, black lace knickers and high heels. Her hand wavered in front of him holding a key. 'What the... hell... fuck... you... here... left me.'

'You not make sense. Get out of way and I open door.'

He staggered thankfully into the darkness of his house and made to go up to his mattress. He was too tired to kill her now but he would later. She followed him. He saw that her lipstick was smudged.

'Jowow. Where you go? Where is the shit? I need joint.'

'Fuck off.'

'Ah Jowow. Be nice to beautiful Sashinha.'

João took off his damp clothes and crawled onto his mattress. He heard her rummaging in his clothes but that was the last he heard until he heard her screaming.

'Jowow, wake up! Wake up!' He shot up, startled, looking at her paint-white face.

'What the fuck, Sasha. Let me sleep, you bitch. You don't know what I went through last night.'

'Shut up. You already sleep four hours. You left shit on beach?'

'Of course, I left it on the beach. Where else could I leave it? You weren't fucking there,' João shouted.

She was silent and her eyes fell to the floor. João had never seen her look away.

'What is it, Sasha? Tell me.'

She stepped back and looked up at him. 'The police, they all over the beach. Tourist find it. They think it something to do with missing girl.'

João felt the blood drain from his arms that were propping him up. He didn't even have the strength to kill her.

'What girl?'

'You know English girl who disappear from Luz two month ago. You remember there is big reward?'

João nodded. He remembered hearing something about it. 'How do you know?'

'I just come from there. I see them and then Zé tell me.'

He was going to ask what she was doing with Zé but then the magnitude of what had happened hit him and he collapsed back onto the mattress. He would still need to pay Pedro and Ahmad. And he wouldn't be able to put Sasha on a plane back to beautiful Russia. Oh fuck. Asshole tourists.

'Get me a coffee and brandy, Sashinha, while I think of something.'

For once she nodded her head.

9. Battered fish

'Why do we need a licence to put a poster in the window?' Ann said, mopping the mucky orange floor tiles of their fish and chip shop. She noticed that the glass front could do with cleaning but she didn't have time. It was 9.45 a.m. and they opened at ten. A nice English man had asked them to put a poster in the window advertising a book he had written about the Algarve. Ann had said, 'yes' but yesterday Dave's mate had, apparently, told Dave that they couldn't.

'I don't know why, love. He just said that the *Câmara* wouldn't allow it without a licence,' Dave, her husband, replied and clicked on the fryers and the lights for the counters. 'You've missed a bit,' he added, pointing to the corner.

'I haven't finished yet. But that's the most bloody ridiculous thing I've ever heard,' Ann said, wringing out the mop in the bucket. 'No one said anything about the poster of the missing girl.'

'That was because it wasn't advertising anything.'

'They were advertising a bloody reward of 10,000 euros!' Ann said.

'I dunno then. But why are you surprised?' Dave said. 'Everything is a bloody nightmare here. Pass me that cloth, will you, love?'

Ann didn't reply. She knew Dave was finding it hard living in the Algarve. They both were. It wasn't the actual running of the fish and chip shop, it was all the laws that they needed to keep on top of. Last week they had to have a slightly larger extractor fan as the old one, that had worked perfectly well, was five centimetres smaller than it should have been. Of course, they'd had to pay builders to do it and had lost a day's takings. It was the middle of August so every hour counted as it was hardly worth opening in the winter and what with the two thousand euros they were paying a month for the rent, the ten thousand euros they'd already paid for the five-year *trespasse*, the *IVA* on everything, they were struggling. They could have done with finding that little girl, Ann

114

couldn't help thinking. She'd had dreams of bringing the great British tradition to the Algarve, both for the Brits abroad and the Portuguese, while living the life of Riley by the sea in Praia da Rocha. They deserved it – their two kids were grown-up and had their own lives. She and Dave were still only in their forties so there was still time to do things with their life. But, she had to confess, Riley wasn't quite how she'd imagined. Neither was Dave for that matter. As he wiped the glass, she caught him looking at a couple of young girls walking by in high shoes and mini-skirts.

'Are the potatoes ready?' she called to little Pete in the back.

'Almost,' Pete shouted back. She could hear the potato cutter grinding. There had been the cost of the fryers and gadgets as well, all the things needed to kit the shop out. The whole venture had cost them about a hundred grand and they were hardly making a living. Ah well, she thought, taking the bucket through to the back, we have to try things in life. She changed her apron, tied her shoulder length blond hair back with a red scrunchy and put on some lipstick. She couldn't do much about the crow's feet around her eyes or the vertical hyphens above her lips. Still she wasn't bad looking for her age.

The cut potatoes were lying in two large containers filled with water and crates of rapidly defrosting cod, haddock and plaice were piled up on the floor.

'For God's sake get that lot in the freezer,' she said. 'We're not going to need all those.'

'Dave said he was going to see to that,' Pete said, momentarily scowling at her. Bubbles of sweat were already bursting onto his forehead.

She was going to say that Dave said a lot of things but she didn't. He had obviously forgotten as she could hear him making the batter. It wasn't worth making a scene: Pete was the best they'd found. He was quick and he'd only not showed up twice in four months.

'Dave, the fish are melting. How many do you want?' she called to her husband.

'Bring me half a dozen cod, half a dozen haddock and a couple of plaice, will you, love.'

Ann got three trays and quickly dipped the fish into flour and took them to Dave. Pete followed with a couple of buckets of cut potatoes.

'There's people waiting already.' She waved to them and shouted she would be out in a minute before realising that they were Portuguese. Oh dear, she still didn't even have a menu in Portuguese. Dave chucked in the chips and the oil hissed and stirred like sleeping snakes, rudely awakened.

She went outside where there were six tables on the small paved terrace area in between the shop and the pedestrian way. Glass wind breakers and a few palms with large skinny hands growing out of pots separated their terrace from the two neighbouring restaurants. Two elderly people sat, overdressed, uncomfortably looking around. The man wore a cap and a dark waistcoat over a white shirt, the woman was in a long navy skirt, a short-sleeve nylon blouse, tanned tights and flat black shoes. They looked like they were on a pilgrimage from the last century. The man put on a pair of glasses as she approached.

'Good morning. *Bom dia*,' she said, handing them the menu card.

'*Bom dia*,' the man began, and then thundered ahead in Portuguese. Ann didn't have a clue what he was saying. She held up her hands and smiled deeply.

'I'm sorry!' she said, 'English?'

The man shook his head, still speaking Portuguese, looking at his wife. She didn't say anything but glared at the menu and then at Ann expectantly. Ann opened her hands like the palm trees in the pots and twisted her mouth into a question mark. The man continued speaking to her and then, finally, put the menu down on the table, touched his wife's arm and the two got up and left.

Ann was left standing with the menus and a heavy heart. She knew Dave was watching her from the fryers. She wanted to learn Portuguese but it was so hard. She'd bought all the tapes and books but buying them was not enough. She had thought about going to a language school, or to the lessons the *Câmara* offered for foreigners, but they couldn't afford to pay for someone to work while she was out. She walked back into the shop where Dave was taking the chips out of the fryer.

'Don't worry,' Dave said, banging oil from the chips. 'You did your best. It's not your fault.'

Ann felt close to tears; her best didn't seem even remotely worthwhile.

'We've been here over a year, Dave,' she said. 'And I don't even understand what people want. I must learn.'

'Ah, what's the big deal, love. Most people speak English.'

'But we are in their country, Dave.'

'But we are English, Ann.'

Ann felt uncomfortable with his answer but she didn't say anything. Just because they were English did that mean they should expect everyone to speak English? They expected everyone to speak English in England – and many didn't – but they weren't in England. She resolved to try to learn the language during the afternoons when they weren't quite so busy.

Just then a large athletic man with short dark hair swept into the shop, followed by three gigantic young women, all dressed up to the nines in high heels, shorts or short skirts and make-up. The man looked older – maybe he was a father of one of them. Or a manager. Or a pimp.

'Hey, good morning, do you do proper English fish and chips?' the man asked in an American accent.

'We do,' Ann said. 'Would you like to sit outside or take-away?'

'Are they the big, fat, soggy chips?' one of the girls asked, in a southern accent. She had dark hair pulled off her face and round translucent blue-sky eyes. The others laughed at her. The man rolled his eyes playfully. He was just slightly taller than she was.

'They are. Just like you'd get at home,' Dave said, grabbing a wooden fork and passing her one.

Ann couldn't help noticing Dave's mouth almost salivating as she took it gratefully. With his balding head and bulging waist, he looked ridiculous.

'She's been going on about English fish and chips for four hours,' the man explained, smiling. He had soft brown eyes – too kind for a pimp, a manager or a father. 'A burger wouldn't do, it had to be fish and chips. Well, babe, how is it?'

'Yum!' she said, and both the man and Dave smiled. 'That's just what I want. Have you got any rolls as well?'

Ann nodded.

'We can have chip butties.'

'They'll make you fat,' the man said.

'I don't care,' she replied, playfully knocking him with her handbag.

'Do you want to sit down?' Ann reiterated.

'No, let's have take-aways and go and sit by the sea!' one of the other girls said. She seemed a little younger, although it was hard to tell.

'It would be nice to sit down,' the other older one said. She had long, blonde straight hair. 'I'm knackered. Charlotte, what do you want?'

'Let's sit down, I'm knackered too.'

They piled out of the shop. Dave's eyes drooled after them. Even little Pete was peering in from the back.

'Lucky bastard,' Dave muttered.

'Huh!' Ann said, as she collected up some menus. Dave never used to be like that. What was it with middle-aged men? They would run off with the first woman who winked at them as long as she was younger. And buy them whatever they wanted. When that had happened to Elaine, a friend of hers, a couple of months ago, Dave had told her that it was because Mark, the husband, had worked hard for twenty years, supporting the family, raising the kids and now felt he deserved to enjoy life a bit. Ann hadn't said anything – it seemed too obvious to state that surely bringing a family up together was the most joyous thing anyone could do. Poor Elaine. She said that she felt as if her home had been torn down, as if she were walking barefoot through the rubble of what had once been her life. She'd be all right though. Mark was an idiot.

As she handed the menu to the man surrounded by the beautiful girls sitting around the table she tried to imagine his history. She bet there was some hurting wife somewhere – although she probably wasn't barefoot. The guilt usually made the men pay for their wives. Even Mark had left the house to Elaine – not that she said it helped. But Ann bet she would feel differently in a few months' time.

'Are you on holiday or are you living here,' she asked, smiling at them.

'Both,' the man said and laughed. 'The girls here are working.' He seemed to enjoy the look of confusion that her face must have shown. 'They're dancers,' he said.

She nodded and said that that must be fun.

'How long have you been here?' he asked her, leaning back on the chair with his hands behind his head. He was made of confidence.

'About fifteen months,' Ann said.

'Good business?'

'Not bad,' she said. 'Quite hard to find your way around at first but we're getting there.'

118

'Well, you're the only proper fish and chip shop for miles and miles and I know as they've made me drive around looking for hours.'

The sky-blue eyed girl hit him again and the others laughed. The man looked indignant. 'Is that not true?' he asked.

'It is true. We've been looking everywhere. I would like cod and chips and a roll and butter,' the blue-eyed girl said slowly, relishing each word.

The others ordered the same and two litre bottles of fizzy water.

'And salt and vinegar please!' one of them called after her.

'Are they tourists?' Dave asked as she went in.

'No, they're dancers.'

'Dancers? Here?'

'I don't know, I didn't ask.' Ann gave her husband the order, then went out to take more orders from some Brits who were pulling up their chairs – a union jack T-shirt a giveaway.

The other tables quickly filled up and Ann was soon running around with plates of fish and chips, steak and kidney pies and chips, chicken pies, fishcakes, pineapple rings and black pudding. The sun burned through the slits in the covered terraces between theirs and the neighbouring restaurants. If she looked to the right she could see a blanket of blue: the deep blue of the sea against the lighter blue of the sky. Sometimes, she just wanted to wrap herself in that blanket. They'd only spent a whole day on the beach three times in fifteen months, although sometimes she got up early and went for a walk by the sea before breakfast and watched the waves race onto the sand; at times as if they couldn't wait to get to the end of their destination, at other times gingerly creeping up the beach, as if afraid what would happen when they fell through the grains.

'You see, you don't need to speak Portuguese,' Dave said.

He was right. As usual all the rest of the customers were English that morning – apart from the American with the dancers, who left her a fourteen euro tip.

Nevertheless, as soon as the lunchtime rush was over, she sat down in the kitchen at the back, next to the buckets of chips, with her *Survive in Portuguese* and read through the sentences again and again. Then she put a tape into a player and listened and repeated them.

'Christ, Ann, I don't know why you're bothering. There's so much that needs doing. There's people out there waiting for a start.'

'Couldn't you serve them for once,' she said, smiling up at him.

'No, it's your job, love.'

'Well I got you the fish this morning and put the rest in the freezer before they started swimming again.'

'I know, love. But you're much better at serving than I am.'

'You've never tried!' Feeling slightly mean, she put the book down on the chair and went outside to serve them. They wanted beer and chips.

'Sounds like Chinese to me,' Dave joked, nodding with his head towards the tape recorder, as she went back in with the order. She noticed a copy of the Daily Mail folded on the window ledge.

'Do you know Chinese then?' Ann asked, without thinking.

Dave looked at her strangely. 'Don't go getting cocky. It doesn't suit you.'

Ann went back to her book. *'O que é que deseja?'* she said, over and over again. She tried it on some of the customers but they looked at her blankly. 'Just practising,' she explained.

'Shouldn't think you'd need the local lingo here,' one customer said.

'I can just about manage *'Bom dia'* and *'Obrigado'*, said another. 'That's all you need really, isn't it? Show a bit of willing.'

Then one customer actually responded in Portuguese. She said that she wanted *'Só batatas fritas'* and an *'agua'*.

'Obrigada,' said Ann, her heart flapping like a young bird trying to take off.

The woman was tall and dark-haired and could have been Portuguese, but then she spoke English to the guy she was with who looked familiar. Ann vaguely remembered that he had been here before.

Ann explained, 'I'm trying to learn the language, you see.'

'Well done,' the woman said. 'So many people don't bother.'

'Where did you learn?' Ann asked.

'By myself. But we live up in the mountains so not so many people speak English. There's more chance to practise.'

'I'll have steak and kidney pie and chips,' the man said. 'Oh, and a beer.'

The woman challenged him with her eyes but he avoided her by staring at the menu.

120

She went off to get the drinks. Here in Portugal they could sell alcohol. She hadn't been sure if it had been a good idea – after coming out of the pubs in the UK the last thing people needed was a beer with their chips but here, aside from a few rowdy youngsters, it hadn't been a problem. They had decided on only bottled beer and wine. Keep it simple. There were so many other places to go if someone wanted to drink.

As she took the drinks to the young couple, she couldn't help but overhear them. The woman was having a go about him drinking. He'd promised he wouldn't ever drink again after what had happened last time. The man was confidently assuring her that it was different now, he could control it and it was only a beer for God's sake. He promised he wouldn't touch spirits – and he hadn't, had he, apart from one *medronho*? She muttered that it was his life and Ann suspected there was something else coming but she had arrived with the drinks. She felt a bit guilty pouring the beer, but it was only a beer. Everyone liked a little drink now and then, but some people just didn't know when to stop. Maybe he was one of those. Whichever, it looked like another relationship on the rocks, she thought, as she poured the woman her water. So many couples came to the Algarve and split up. She didn't know why. Maybe it was because they were forced to ask too many questions about themselves. Or maybe it was because they had changed their lives so much that they didn't know when to stop.

By the end of the week, Ann had worked her way through the book and it was beginning to stick. She practised on anyone she could find. She tried to speak Portuguese in the Alisuper and in the shops. Everyone spoke back to her in English which was very annoying but she would then ask them how they would say that in Portuguese and repeat it. Soon, the locals were greeting her in Portuguese and although she couldn't get much further than '*Tudo bem*' and the state of the weather, she made more progress in a week than she had in a year. She struggled with the two verbs meaning 'to be': '*Estou bem*' meaning 'I am well' and '*Sou inglesa*' meaning 'I am English'. One was temporary, the other permanent. She wasn't sure if she understood how some things could be permanent. For example, '*Sou casada*' meaning 'I am married' or '*Sou negociante*' (I am a businessman/woman) or '*Sou simpatica*' (I am kind) were permanent. But how could they be permanent when her life may change tomorrow? She may change. Maybe they belonged to a time when these things were forever.

She translated the menu with the help of the woman who ran the newsagents and put a sandwich board outside in Portuguese. Her husband kept asking her why she was bothering but after a few days she didn't bother to answer him as he sat reading his Daily Mail and watching the girls in their bikini tops and shorts from his little stool by the window.

Portugal, and most of southern Europe, took the month of August off and yet still no Portuguese came in. But there were plenty of other nationalities who spoke a spattering of Portuguese and they liked to practise as well. They were busy – Ann busier than others as she was still studying whenever she could, including after work.

'Why are you still doing this?' Dave said, one night when they were in bed. 'You're looking knackered and you have no time for me. And you still haven't needed the language, love.'

'You mean I'm too knackered for sex?' Ann challenged him, looking up from the dictionary. She wanted to know what 'batter' was.

'That as well. But you never want to have a drink after work. You're being boring, love.'

'That's because I don't like to get up with a hangover, Dave. You know that. We'll have more time in the winter to relax.' She turned the page. *Massa crua para fritos*. It seemed a long way of explaining 'batter'.

He grunted and fell asleep, snoring loudly.

Then one day in the beginning of September a group of Portuguese came and sat down, Ann felt her heart thump. There were six people, four adults and two children.

'*Boa tarde*,' she said, handing them the menu.

'*Boa tarde*,' the man said and asked if she could explain how the fish was cooked.

She told him that the fish was put in batter and then fried. She had been practising. They all began talking to each other. Ann didn't understand much. Then the man asked her if she could do two without the batter? Ann thought carefully. Cod in particular often fell apart but she didn't know how to say that. '*Linguado ou eglefim são melhores para fritar.*' Plaice and haddock are better for frying. Permanent. Even if not for long. The group nodded knowingly and ordered four cod and chips, two plaice without batter, and chips, a bottle of red wine and 7-Up.

122

'*Obrigada*,' Ann said.

She wanted to jump over the tables as she walked into the shop, triumphantly waving the order.

'I did it! I did it!' she said.

'Did what, love?'

'Took an order in Portuguese.'

'Well, it can't be that hard.'

Ann felt the elation seep out of her fingers.

Dave must have seen the look on her face as he added, 'I mean, seeing as you've had the menu translated, you know.'

But it was too little too late.

Ann handed him the order, took off her little apron.

'What you doing, love.'

Ann didn't reply. It was near the end of the day – he could cope for once. She walked out of the shop and onto the walkway. She didn't know where she was going. She didn't know where or when she would stop. but her eyes panned upwards to where the seagulls dipped and glided through the sky. She wanted to wrap herself in the blue. She turned left towards the sea, only vaguely aware of her husband calling after her.

10. The singing dog

Günter stopped at the end of the beach and gazed out at the last of the mist evaporating from the sea like departing ghosts. The sun was rising, a pinkish ball, out of the horizon into the baby-blue sky and lit up the white satin sea. He sat on a rock and lit the joint he had prepared before coming out, all the time keeping his eye on Doch swimming in a straight line about twenty metres from the shore. Further down the beach, a fishing boat was coming in from the night's catch and the tractor belched to life before turning towards the sea.

Doch barked as a seagull hovered above him and increased his speed. 'You can't fly, Doch,' Günter said, smiling. Doch's webbed feet weren't much good in the sky, much to Doch's dismay as he turned and swam the flight path of the seagull. Günter whistled at him and Doch turned round and headed to the beach. Günter smoked the rest of his joint and let his mind drift beyond the sea. Here he had found paradise. A world in which there was time to enjoy the sunrise and the beauty of nature, to share suppers and friendships, to love time rather than to find it. Here the world was as it should be – away from the global capitalism that had swept across the world like an oil slick, creating societies rigid with stress, greed, competitiveness and selfishness, a world in which poverty was judged by lack of money rather than spirit. A world which called him a loser. In this small fishing village in the Algarve, poverty was not judged by money and things. Here, he could be himself.

He had long thought it ironic how, traditionally, in all ancient societies, understanding and wisdom were born out of study, meditation and journeys, both physical and mental. The acquisition of goods and money were not what wise people did, from the monks of Tibet and the saddhus of India to the prophets of Islam and Christianity. No religion or philosophy taught that the acquisition of things led to happiness or enlightenment. Of course, food, warmth, clothes and shelter were fundamental and the right of any human being but, beyond that...

Günter's thoughts were grounded by seawater as Doch shook himself. Günter laughed and patted his head. 'You wouldn't like to buy the latest BMW or invest in a half a million euro villa or gold shares, would you, Doch?'

Doch shook his head, barked and sat down next to him, his black eyes burrowing into Günter's. He was called 'Doch' because he always affirmed a point Günter was unsure of. Well, usually.

'Of course not. Look at it!' Günter spread his arms to embrace the sea, the sand, the sky. 'What more could we want?'

Doch jumped up and barked twice.

'*Ja,* okay, a stash of dope and a few good bones would be good, wouldn't they?' He ruffled Doch's black floppy ears and Doch rolled around in the sand, a silly smile revealing his jagged razor sharp teeth.

Some stupid tourists had called the police after finding João's hash on the beach, claiming they thought it might be something to do with the missing girl. Did they think she'd been shrunk into a five-litre bottle? No one in the village could believe anyone could do such a stupid thing. They were Germans as well. Günter had felt ashamed but that was not a new feeling. No one held it against him. Of course, no one had said it was João's, and so no one had been arrested, but everyone knew it was his because as soon as the GNR had gone, João had practically single-handedly dug up the beach just to check that they really had taken it.

'Come on then, Doch. *Frühstück.*'

Doch barked and ran ahead, leaping up at the squawking seagulls. Günter followed, slowly, enjoying the creases his boots made in the smooth sand. The seagulls around the fishing boat were making Doch dizzy with excitement and frustration, his sole aim in life seemed to be to chase seagulls. Once he had caught one, its broken wing twisted out of his mouth, its pale blue eyes open but dead. Doch had dropped it on the sand and nudged it with his nose, barked at it, but when it didn't get up he trotted off. Like life, the fun was in the journey, not the destination.

Günter put Doch on a lead as they went past Jorge's fishing boat, the *Fica Bem.* Little Mário was there but he was looking out to sea rather than at the fish being unloaded. He was there nearly every morning, as if waiting for his father to return. Poor Mário. But he wouldn't be the first to lose his father – fathers were fairly unreliable creatures. If they didn't die they tended to disappear somehow. Günter's own had run off with another woman when he was still a baby. His mother told him his father had used to see him until he was about three but then he had started a family with the other woman and had never made contact since. Günter had no memory of him and couldn't say he missed him as he had never known him. Then, he himself had left a woman pregnant twenty-five years ago. He didn't know if it had been a boy or girl, or if he or she were still alive. He hoped he had never been missed and he was almost sure he hadn't been. But Mário had been that bit older: he had known what he had lost – and that was always harder.

'*Bom dia*, Günter,' Jorge called.

'*Bom dia.*'

'*Tudo bem?*'

'*Mais ou menos.* Not too much work at the moment.'

'Then I take you fishing!'

'*Ja gut!*'

More 'bom dias' were exchanged with the old fishermen sitting on the bench, leaning on sticks, dressed in their caps. It was a morning ritual. Günter crossed the square and sat down at the empty *pastelaria* for a coffee. It was the beginning of September and the tide had taken away many of the tourists. He looked around for Paul who had said that he needed him to do some painting but there was no sign of him. Workers were re-laying the *calçada* by hand – tap, tap, tap. It was the third time they'd dug it up and relaid it. Günter smiled. Only here (or in the old USSR) could that happen.

He picked up the *Correio da Manhã* and flicked through four pages about the missing girl. If he understood, the parents were now being accused of hiding the body after an accidental death. Günter turned over. No doubt tomorrow there would be another theory. The next page announced that Bin Laden was alive, free and making videos and that Afghanistan was busy producing opium again. Orwell came to mind.

Esmeralda, the owner's wife, brought him a *bica* and Doch a bowl of water. She also brought Doch some leftovers from the previous night. Günter ordered himself a *bifana*. That would see him through until the evening.

Günter sat there for an hour but Paul didn't show up and no one called him. He only had three euros and fifty-seven cents but he wasn't worried: something would turn up. If not, they could always busk. He paid and went back to the ruin where he had set up camp in the spring. It had a broken door which led to a passageway with a room on either side, both with the roof intact. Günter had chosen the room on the right to inhabit as the wall in the other room had a large crack that went from roof to floor and then forked like lightning. The window frames had long rotted but Günter had draped an old curtain in front of the window. He had found a mattress to sleep on, a little table and two chairs on the *lixo*, and he had a sleeping bag. He'd also found a bookcase that was now full of books, a calor gas stove, some pots and pans and he had built a makeshift barbecue outside. He even had a CD ghetto blaster and his guitar was propped up in the corner. He had everything he needed.

Everyone knew he stayed there, but no one said anything. A couple of locals had warned him that it would be better not to stay in the winter because it wouldn't take much to topple it over. Every winter a few more roofs caved in. Günter wasn't too concerned: once the tourists were gone at the end of this month he would be able to rent a room.

Doch went to sit on his blankets and Günter hooked back his curtain to let in some sunlight and sat down at the table and rolled another little joint. Then he opened a book on Marx and Engels in English that an English woman had given him yesterday. She was, or had been, a school teacher and had an apartment here. Günter didn't know her very well, but she had suddenly become quite friendly yesterday. He suspected she was quite straight like most of the island monkeys but her interest in him had visibly doubled when he told her he had a degree in politics. Then the book had appeared.

Günter had written a dissertation on political ideology and although he wouldn't strictly call himself a Marxist, it was obvious to him that more people should study Marx and learn about the dangers of the capitalist system. Of course it was non-sustainable and Günter was continually amazed by the fact that people didn't see it. The bigger fish were getting bigger and fatter every day as the bigger companies swallowed up the smaller ones. According to Marx, a diminishing number of capitalists gain from the benefits of improved industrialisation, while the workers are made increasingly dependent and desperate, unable to get off the treadmill. You only had to look at the poor bastards who came to this fishing village to chill out for a few days. They may have a

127

house and a car, but they looked half-dead when they arrived on the beach. And there were those who were even worse off. Marx underlined that the price of a commodity should be the remuneration of the work to produce it, but in a capitalist society this can never be so because competition amongst the workers makes them accept less than their due, thus the poorer get poorer. His solution, of course, was the abolition of private property and then redistribution of work and production. 'From everyone according to his faculties, to everyone according to his needs,' which was perhaps naïve but that didn't diminish the powerful critique of capitalism. At some point, Günter thought – and some point in the near future – capitalism would implode. What would happen when there were no more medium fish to eat? The bigger fish would need to be fed by the State, or else they would die taking with them millions of little fish who were dependent on them, not only in their countries but also globally as it was now a global economy. The financial world would collapse.

'Hey Günter? Are you there?'

Doch began barking.

Günter went to the door and found the English woman who had given him the book, Sarah, walking along the trodden path to the wasteland towards him.

'Hallo Sarah.'

'Hey, how are you? Hey Dog.'

'Doch.'

'Ah, Dock.' She ruffled his ears anyway. He jumped around her.

'I am very good. I was just looking at the book you gave me yesterday. It is a Russian publication.'

'Yes, I studied in Russia.'

Günter raised his eyebrows. Maybe she wasn't such an island monkey.

'Russian and French,' she clarified. 'Language and literature. I lived in Moscow for a year during the Gorbachev days.'

'The last president of the Soviet Union.'

'The ghost president of a ghost state.' She smiled. She had green eyes and her now white hair shone almost angelically.

'Sadly.'

'Maybe. It was pretty bloody miserable though – unless you were a Party member, of course. It had its own elite, I'm afraid. And it was so corrupt. The only way of getting a table in a restaurant was bribery – preferably dollars – and then more bribery to get something to eat. Even then you didn't have a choice.' She smiled.

'*Ja, ja*, it was the same in East Germany.'

'Of course. And then there were the prefab houses. I lived in one for a year and it was truly depressing. It wasn't a beautiful world. Who was it who said that the reason why there is so much crime in America is because they have ugly wallpaper?'

Günter shook his head. He had never heard this before but there was a certain truth to it.

'I can't remember but the fact remains that we need beauty in our lives. Anyway, would you like to go for a coffee? I'm on my way to the beach so we could go to one of the beautiful beach cafes if you like? My treat.'

'Thank you,' said Günter. 'I think it is time for beer. Come on then, Doch. This nice lady will buy us a drink.'

'GOON-TA! GOON-TA!'

He looked up and saw Sasha waving frantically at him from the road. He waved back.

'WAIT! I COME!'

'Who is that?'

'That's Sasha, the mad Russian. Have you not met her?'

'No, not yet.'

Sasha bobbed up and down through the grass as she half ran, half ambled along the path.

'Goonta, you have something I smoke?'

'Sasha, this is Sarah. Sarah knows Russian.'

'Hello. Russian? You know me? Goonta, this is emergency. I need the dope for Jowow. He very sick.'

'I have some, but not much.' Günter turned and went back into his ruin. He broke off a crumb and took it to Sasha to find her blabbing away to Sarah in Russian.

'Why you not tell me she speak Russian,' Sasha said accusingly.

Günter shrugged and handed her the little bit of dope. 'What is wrong with him?'

'With who?'

'João.'

'Oh I think he has depression. He says he in black hole. I tell him to go outside but he say the light will kill him. And also Pedro try to kill him because he owe him money.'

Günter smiled to himself. João owed everyone money – even him. He was going to invite them round later but then remembered that he now had less than two euros. But he did have a bottle of Capataz.

'Maybe tell him to come round when the sun sets for the glass of *vinho*.'

'Okay, Goonta. Good. *Ciao*.'

Sasha turned and fled once more over the wasteland.

'She is mad,' Sarah said. 'Does she work here?'

'Who knows? She has bad, how do you say, repute?'

'Reputation.'

'Reputation. Some say she's a prostitute and supports João, others say that João supports her. It doesn't matter. She's nice, very funny.' Günter put Doch on a lead.

'She said that some German robbed them of their fortune. What happened?'

Günter laughed and, as they went to the *pastelaria,* he told her about the dope found on the beach. They crossed over the little bridge and passed the boats crashed out on the beach while the fishermen huddled in the shade staring out to sea. Jorge was talking to a tourist dressed in polished shoes, pressed trousers and white short-sleeve shirt. Jorge nodded at Günter and Sarah and Günter exchanged more 'bom dias' with the resting fishermen and then crossed onto the walkway that went to the last little wooden restaurant. They sat down at a table on the promenade. Sarah arranged the umbrella and she ordered a coffee and a beer for him.

'They still haven't found that little girl,' Sarah said, gazing at the beach where children were absorbed in building sand castles. 'It's amazing when the whole world is looking for her.'

Günter shrugged. 'They also not find Osama Bin Laden.'

'Yeah but many people are probably hiding him.'

'Perhaps many people are hiding her. Or maybe they are both dead.'

'Maybe. Have you heard, they're saying now that the mother may have accidentally killed her by giving her a sleeping tablet or something and covered up the evidence. What mother would do that? It's outrageous.'

Günter didn't say anything. It was an emotive issue with the Brits. Claudia brought them their drinks and a bowl of water for Doch.

'Well, what do you think then?' Sarah prodded.

'What I think? I know that it wasn't João and Sasha although I think it did give them some ideas as they were hanging about on

130

the beach last week looking for a child they could kidnap so that they could get the reward.'

Sarah laughed. 'But did the police do a lot here? You know in the UK they are saying that they aren't doing enough.'

'I think they use the whole police force in Portugal, millions of taxpayers' money, and many people working extraordinary time and for no pay. Everyone I know was pulled over and questioned. Every van was stopped and searched. You must see all the posters, the rewards, the newspapers, the news?'

'Really? They never say that in England.'

'You know what your tabloid press is like.'

'I guess. What do you think to the whole affair?'

'I think, as I believe Stalin said, that when a hundred thousand people die it is a statistic, but when a little girl disappears it is a tragedy.'

'That's true.'

'You know every day hundreds of children disappear.'

'Yes, of course. That doesn't make it any less of a tragedy though.'

They fell silent and gazed out to sea. The sun was higher now, the sea darker and deeper, glossy and textured like an oil painting against the matt water colour of the sky. One thing that always amazed Günter was how the sea constantly changed. There were as many variants as there were colours and patterns. Winds, clouds, tides, seasons and time all acted on the seascape to ensure that no two days were ever the same, no two hours and no two minutes.

'It's beautiful,' Sarah whispered. 'Do you think you'll stay?'

'*Ja*, for now. I do not want to go back to Germany. The people of northern Europe have lost their lives and their minds. They live crazy mad lives working, working, working. They are unhappy and too stupid to understand why.'

'What, everyone?' Sarah smiled at him.

'No, not everyone. But nearly.'

'Well, it's the way society has progressed, isn't it? We need to make a living to survive. We need to work because we need money.'

'Yes, because of capitalism. It is the big ugly machine which, once started, can not be stopped without throwing the world into chaos. But it will end soon.'

'I doubt it! Communism's the one that failed, remember.'

'*Ja,* because countries like Russia make many mistakes. But look at the capitalist world today. It is out of control. The governments need to step in to take over all the big companies, particularly the banks, because they will bankrupt the world.'

Sarah laughed. 'That's a bit strong. How could they do that?'

'Because they lend too much credit. One day, people find that they can not pay their *hipoteca*, how do you say, mortgage, because they lose their job because there is too much competition. The banks borrow more from themselves but as the people can not find work they can not spend and so the economy slows down. More people are unemployed because they are not needed in the jobs because no one is buying anything and so more and more people can not pay the debts. More people draw money from their banks. Suddenly the banks do not have enough money. And bang-bang! Capitalism destroys the world.'

'That's a bit extreme!'

'*Ja,* you see. It happens.'

'Do you want another beer?'

'Sure, but I'm afraid I have no money.'

'Don't worry, the banks still have money for now. Let me get them.' Sarah called Claudia and pointed to their glasses and smiled. 'You really have no money?'

'I have just over one euro.'

Sarah laughed. 'Nothing more?'

'No.'

'No savings? No nothing? God, I don't how you live.'

'Something always shows up. I have work at the campsite next week. And we give concerts if all else fails, don't we Doch?'

Günter nodded at Doch and he barked.

'What kind of concerts?' Sarah asked.

'I play the guitar and Doch sings. You must come along one day.'

'I will. Would you like a loan? I am here until next week.'

'Thank you but it is not necessary.'

'Why don't you sign on the dole? You have good social security in Germany, don't you?'

'Because I would have to live there. I would rather be here. Here I am free.'

'That's admirable.'

Claudia brought the beers and they clinked glasses, drank to freedom and gazed once more at the horizon, that illusionary line.

After Sarah had gone to the beach, Günter went to the public tap in the square and filled up two five-litre water bottles and left them outside his door in the sun and spent the afternoon sitting outside on a chair reading the book Sarah had given him. He chose to read a speech given by Engels at the graveside of Karl Marx. It was hard going in English and he found himself looking up words in his dictionary. 'Marx was the best hated and most *calumniated* man of his time' – 'the most slandered' according to his dictionary. Günter rolled the word round on his tongue for a while. 'To calumniate', a transitive verb, 'calumniation', 'calumniator', singing each word. Doch barked excitedly.

'*Ja,* good idea, Doch.' He picked up his guitar. 'Marx says that we should have food, drink, shelter and clothing before the pursuit of politics, science, art and religion so what are we waiting for?'

Doch barked that he was ready so they sauntered to the seafront where Günter opened his guitar case, took out his guitar and began with some Dylan songs. As soon as he hit the high notes, Doch joined in. A crowd soon gathered as Günter sang and Doch howled. People clapped appreciatively and a few euro coins rolled into the case. After about half an hour, they ended with 'Mr Tambourine Man'. Günter bowed, scooped up the coins and put away his guitar. He had enough money for today. Then he went to the shop to buy some bread, ham, tomatoes and he treated Doch to a tin of Pedigree, *sabor galinha.* He was thirsty after all that singing so he called in at the *pastelaria* for a beer. There was no sign of João or his depression. Or Paul. Maybe he would call tomorrow. Not that it mattered now. He had enough for today.

Günter sat outside and drank his beer watching a few tourists go back to their apartments to shower and change before heading out to the restaurants. For a moment, Günter thought how nice it would be to have a hot shower, a big meal in a restaurant, but then remembered how he would have to live for the rest of the 351 days a year and immediately felt grateful for being able to live here every day. Besides, his water bottles would be hot by now.

He went back to his ruin and showered in the bushes with his five-litre bottles of warm water. No one could see him from the road. He dried almost instantly in the still warm rays and put on a clean shirt. Then he opened the tin of Pedigree and gave Doch his dinner. He was about to make himself a ham sandwich when he heard voices near the ruin.

He went to the door and saw Jorge and Zé coming across. Jorge was carrying a bucket, Zé a packet of charcoal and a bottle of wine.

'*Olá* Günter. We have *jantar,*' Jorge shouted.

As he got closer, Günter could see fish tails peeping over the top of the bucket. 'We make barbecue!'

Günter smiled. This could only happen here. He opened the bottle of Capataz while Jorge got the barbecue going. Zé prepared the fish. His mobile rang and it was Paul calling about some painting work for tomorrow. He agreed to be there at 10 a.m..

'So no work tonight, Zé?' Günter asked, pouring out the Capataz into three empty honey jars. Zé was a waiter in the Paraíso, the

134

biggest restaurant in the village. He was a young man, twenty-five or so. He had his life ahead of him.

'No, tonight is holiday.'

'He has the depression,' Jorge called out. 'He fell in love with the *bife* girl six months ago and didn't realise it until she left. Now, every night he is miserable as hell.'

'Ah. I remember. Zoe?'

Zé nodded.

'I talk to her one day. She was nice – an English teacher. But maybe she comes back. You know everyone who comes here always comes back,' Günter said.

'You think so?' Zé's dark eyes almost cried.

'*Ja,* of course. Why don't you text her?'

'I don't have the number.'

'I have.' Günter found the number on his mobile phone and showed it to Zé. Zé's hands shook as he thumbed in the number to his own phone.

The smell of barbecuing fish filled the darkening sky and the warmth of the wine replaced the cooling day. The Capataz slipped down almost unnoticeably and Günter soon found himself opening another bottle as they sat down to enjoy the fish and bread. The fish was exquisite, soft yet succulent, salty yet sweet.

'You know I have tourist man come to talk to me today when I am sitting with the older fishermen in the square – just after you come,' Jorge said. 'He says he is banker in London. He tells me I should borrow the money from the bank to buy a bigger boat that catch more fish. Then when I make more money I should buy another one. And another one. I should employ people to work for me and catch more fish and make more money. "Okay, and then what?" I ask. "Well, eventually," he says, "after say twenty years, you'd be rich and able to retire and watch the world go by." "It's a good idea," I say, "but what the fuck do you think I'm doing now?"'

Günter opened his mouth and roared with laughter. 'You say that?'

Jorge winked at him.

'The capitalists always worry about the future,' said Günter. 'And so they should because one day soon the bubble will burst and those bankers will get seasick,' Günter said and as he said this he knew it with all his heart that it was true. Maybe it had already started.

He poured more wine and then got his guitar. He strummed a few chords, enjoying the moment of having eaten well, being with friends and drinking wine under a sparkling starry night and then began to sing 'The Internationale' in German. Doch immediately joined in while Jorge and Zé held up their glasses and sang in Portuguese. Footsteps made their way through the dried grasses and Russian words sliced through the air as Sasha and João appeared.

'Why you sing that shit song?' Sasha shouted. 'You want to know what it like to live in communist country. I tell you. It shit.'

11. Worn-out boots

'You need to take a ticket,' Rita shouted at the old man who had just hobbled into the Centro de Saúde with a stick as knobbly as his knees. It looked like he had walked from the Alentejo, the soles of his old leather boots flapped open thirstily. She just knew he wouldn't be able to write and she would have to fill in all the forms for him. Where was Patrícia? It was almost four and Rita should be leaving. She had promised to take her mother to the mountains, but she couldn't leave while the waiting room heaved with thirty-two heavy hearts and only one doctor and two nurses to see them all.

The man looked at the ticket machine in confusion. Rita sighed loudly but, fortunately, another patient got up and showed him how to press the button. The man ripped off the ticket and held it up as he studied the numbers. Rita could see it was upside down. This was going to be useless.

'Come here,' she said, holding up her arm and bending her four fingers towards her.

The man hobbled over.

'What can I do for you?'

'I don't feel good. My stomach. I have too many pains.'

'So you would like to see a doctor?'

The man nodded, his face like a wire scourer. His dark eyes had sunk like holes in sand, gradually filling in.

'Do you have your *Cartão Utente*?'

The man produced his ID card.

'This is not your *Cartão Utente*. Do you have anything else?'

The man shook his head.

'Where do you live?'

The man shrugged.

'Where did you last go to see a doctor?'

'I never see a doctor.'

'Well, then you need to go to the *Finanças* to get your *Cartão Utente*. Oh, sit down,' she said. She would have a word with

137

Doctor Ferreira and maybe he would see him quickly without doing the paperwork.

'Number 412,' Rita shouted. A young girl of about seventeen stood up. 'Go through there and to the room on the left. The doctor will see you in a minute.'

The nurse came in and asked for Dona Louisa Saraiva and an elderly woman wearing a cotton hat and woollen coat got up, leaving her husband buried in a book. She nudged his foot as she went by. He stared after her, his brow scrunched up, as she disappeared through the opaque doors.

Rita sighed and bent down under the counter and picked up a donut. She'd hardly had time for lunch. She never stopped and she was feeling tired of it all. But, at least, in a couple of years' time she would have a semi-decent pension. She was one of the lucky ones. Life was even harder for the old people in the Algarve. They had laboured all their lives, dig-dig-digging the land, sowing seeds, planting, pruning, harvesting, digging again, repairing their houses ravaged by the wind, rain and sun, looking after animals, making bread, making *medronho*, making *presunto*, taking their products to markets... It was never ending. They'd had no time to go to school and that old fascist dictator hadn't encouraged them. They had worked themselves into the ground and had little more than a pile of rubble to show for it as their houses slowly fell down and there was no new money to repair them. Many were now alone because their families had died or moved away.

She knew; she had grown up in the mountains of Monchique and remembered the wet mattress she had had to share with her sister, the cold rooms and the smoky kitchen that used to make her eyes red. There had been no hot water, no bathroom, no heating. She used to have to walk over an hour to get to the school up the mountain. Despite what her mother rambled on about, it wasn't an idyllic or harmonious world. In those days there were a dozen families, fifty-odd inhabitants in the hamlet who would gossip about each other, argue about who had the most irrigation time. She even remembered families denouncing each other to the PIDE. This was the world her mother had clung onto for so long; they'd practically had to kidnap her to bring her to civilisation.

Rita's mother was one of the lucky ones: she had family who would look after her in Portimão. Not that she appreciated it. She was now living with Rita and her husband, João, as her sister-in-law, Alicia, couldn't cope with her mother's moaning about

138

Alicia's *calde verde* tasting like dishwater and the vegetables not being real. She had kept leaving the house and wandering around Portimão in search of fresh air, claiming that the streets were clogged up with bad breath. Alicia had welcomed the company at first but, after a week, she claimed her mother was impossible so she had moved in with Rita and her husband. Now, her husband was looking after her as they still needed Rita's income from the Centro de Saúde to survive. Rita had been ecstatic when the estate agent had told her he'd found a buyer for her mother's house in the mountains. The money would help them make ends meet and help her son, Rui, who was studying in Coimbra to be an architect, and her nieces who also now had their own lives in Lisbon. She hadn't told her mother yet though and she didn't think she'd take the news too well. This weekend may be her last chance to stay in the mountains. Even if the sale didn't go through it was the end of September and the rains would come soon. They had been up most Sundays during the summer but only for the day as Rita didn't like staying there overnight. Her mother had kept saying she needed to speak to the foreigners but they were never there.

A loud bang brought her back to the reception desk as someone tried to ram through the doors. *Fogo,* she muttered, wiping the sugary crumbs from her mouth. A middle-aged man was being half carried, half dragged through the entrance by a tall young woman in high shoes, a red mini skirt and black tights with a white powdered face, black kohl around the eyes and red lipstick. She came straight to the desk and spoke to her in heavily accented Portuguese.

'You help him. He need doctor. He very sick.'

'Your *cartão utente* please,' she asked the man who was swaying slowly. He had leaking blue eyes giving his normally dark face a greyish hue.

'This is emergency and you want to do paperwork! He very sick. Maybe he die.'

'Here,' the man said, placing a very well-used *cartão utente* on the balcony. The edges were all jagged as if he'd used it to try to cut things with it. Or had chewed it.

Rita stared at the man. If it was an emergency he should go to the hospital and it was up to her to tell them.

'What is wrong?' she asked.

'He have black hole inside. He not eat. He not smoke. He not drink. He hardly talk. Look at him. He ghost.'

Rita almost smiled. She didn't think it was an emergency – unless he had overdosed on something.

'Has he taken drugs?' she asked.

'No! Drugs, no. He no money.'

'Fill this in,' she said. 'Number 413,' she called as the young girl came out.

'We see doctor now?' the woman asked.

'No, you must take a ticket and wait your turn. The doctor will see him as soon as he can.'

The woman led the man away muttering that this would never happen in Russia. Rita was tempted to tell her that she should go back there then but, of course, she didn't. But, really, she didn't think it fair that drug addicts and alcoholics used up the doctor's time when it was their own doing while hundreds of other people were suffering through no fault of their own.

Her mobile rang. It was João. She answered it and told him that she couldn't talk. The reception phone started ringing.

'We're waiting in the car,' João said. 'Where are you?'

'I'll be home soon,' she said, snapping the phone shut and answering the other phone to make an appointment for a Dona Fernandes in four weeks' time at the end of October – the next available slot.

Where was Patrícia? It was nearly quarter past. The old lady came out together with the doctor. Rita saw Doctor Ferreira look around the waiting room and almost heard his screams. She explained about the old man who had no *cartão utente* and he agreed to see him at some point. The other doctor, Doctor Nunes, wouldn't have done.

'Number 414,' she called.

She finally left at 5 p.m., an hour later than she should have done and, of course, there would be no extra pay. Patrícia had arrived running, full of apologies; her car hadn't started so she had to take the bus and the bus didn't come. Rita lived within walking distance. She normally enjoyed the walk and often called in for a *galão* and a *pastel de nata* on her way home at her favourite *pastelaria*, but today she hurried back to their apartment block to find her mother and João still sitting in the old white Renault Clio. Her mother was packed up in the back like an old china doll, her shoulder length grey and white streaked hair held off her face by a green hair slide.

140

João didn't bother to get out the car to kiss her, but simply said, 'There you are. We've been waiting an hour.'

'I'm sorry, Patrícia was late.'

Then her mother opened the car door.

'I'm tired of sitting here. I need to wee,' she said.

'*Olá Mãe*, I'm almost ready. Can't you hold on a bit longer?'

'No.'

'Okay, then we'll go to the bathroom. I should change anyway.'

They all took the lift up to the fourth floor. Rita suddenly felt tired and hungry. It would be better to go the next morning but João had got everything ready. It would mean unpacking the car.

Her mother went to the bathroom while Rita went into the kitchen and opened the fridge and crammed two *sonhos* into her mouth. She ignored João's look. He was watching her impatiently.

'You haven't told her, have you?' she asked.

'What?'

'About the offer for the house?'

'No, of course not. I don't think we should say anything. She told me she was going to stay there. She said the nice young neighbours would look after her.'

'Oh dear.'

Still chewing, Rita went into the bedroom and changed her clothes into something more comfortable and warm. It would be cold up in the mountains when they arrived. By the time she was ready, her mother was no longer in the bathroom.

'Where is she?' she asked João, who had moved into the lounge and had switched on the news. The accused parents of the missing girl were saying something but she didn't have time to read the subtitles as João was pointing to her mother's bedroom.

'*Mãe?*' she called. 'Are you ready?'

Her mother was lying on her back on the bed, a blanket pulled over her, a wooden cross and the picture of São Sebastian above her. Rita could see her worn-out, ankle length, faded leather boots poking out the bottom of the blanket. Her mother had had them forever. They were coarse people, her mother's generation, they wouldn't dream of taking off their boots in the house, they would even keep them on in bed sometimes. Rita was going to take them off for her, but decided against it. She didn't want to upset her any more. A black and white photo of her grandmother, mother, her father, Rita and her sister, with the donkey in the background, leaned back on the bedside table in a silver frame. Rita must have only been three or four. She could almost smell the damp house from the faded photo. Rita and her sister were barefoot.

'*Mãe?* Are you all right? Let's go.'

'I don't much feel like it, *filha*. The car, you know, makes me feel sick and I already spend one hour in it. My stomach hurts.'

'But it wasn't moving, *Mãe!*'

'I know but it still makes me feel sick. Can we go tomorrow and then I will stay there? The nice foreigners will look after me.'

'I doubt it, *Mãe*, they have their own lives. And there'll be no doctor to see about your back.' Rita stroked her mother's hand. Dark contours and spots branded the loose skin. Rita didn't like the way this conversation was going.

'They've been looking after Martinho. I need to see him. I need to get him back.'

Rita had no idea what she was on about. Her father had been dead for fifteen years. She felt her mother's forehead: she didn't feel hot but her dark beady eyes looked like they were seeing things she wasn't.

'You can see the foreigners tonight when we go, but you must come back. Remember you have an appointment on Tuesday about your stomach pains.'

'Pah. What use are doctors? When your time's up, your time's up. And I'd rather die in my mountains than in this coffin.'

Rita used her years of patience to swallow the fact that her mother was calling her home a coffin but, at the same time, she couldn't stop the words that gushed out.

'*Mãe,* I think you should know. The estate agent, the man who sells houses, has found you a buyer. We need the money, *Mãe,* to look after you and the rest of the family. So I think we should all go to the mountains now to make the most of it this weekend. What do you say?'

Her mother's mouth fell open ever so slightly and Rita immediately regretted saying anything.

'Of course, we won't go through with it if you don't want,' she added, she knew, belatedly.

'You could have waited until I left my boots,' she said and turned over so that her back was facing Rita.

'Oh *Mãe,* you may live for another five years, another twenty years even! What would we do then?'

'I won't,' the old lady said.

'Can we please go now?'

But her mother had pulled the blanket up around her chin and closed her eyes.

'Please, *Mãe.* The weather forecast is good. Let's go and spend one last wonderful weekend in the mountains.'

'I don't feel so good, *filha.*'

Rita sighed. 'Okay, *Mãe.* I'll go and get you something to eat.'

'I don't want anything.'

Rita went back into the lounge where João was still watching the news. She sat down, exhausted. She was tired from trying so hard to please everyone.

'She won't go,' Rita said.

'You told her?' João said.

Rita nodded.

'We'll never get her to go now.'

'I know. She says she's not feeling well. Says she is sick of the car.'

'Then we may as well unpack.'

They went down to the car and carried up a cool box full of food, two large overnight bags, and several carrier bags containing Seven-Up and Coca-Cola, *bolos* and crisps. João had gone to a lot of trouble to remember everything. Rita unpacked the kitchen things and heated up some vegetable soup for everyone. She put a bowl on a tray and went to take it to her mother. She would explain to her that they would go to the mountains tomorrow and that, if her mother wanted, she would cancel the buyer. On reflection, maybe Rita had acted in haste. After all, it was unlikely that her mother would be with them for another year, let alone twenty.

As she pushed open the door, she could see her mother had climbed into bed beneath the blankets. Her mouth was open slightly and her wiry white hair straggled her face. Rita blinked tears as she saw that her mother had taken off her boots and had carefully placed them by the foot of the bed, facing the door.

12. Departure

'Ed, the problem is you've spent almost as much as the houses are going to cost! And all we've got are five possibilities. It's October for Christ's sake. You've been there for six months! Now, you've gotta get your ass back to London and do some work to cover all this. We can not, as a company, sustain these expenses that you're costing us.'

Ed held the cell phone away from his ear and felt his eyes roll around the sockets. Charlotte gazed at him sympathetically as she dipped a prawn in the garlic sauce. She was looking stunning as ever in a white shirt moulded onto her breasts, and blue jeans that hugged her long legs. Her arms and face were tanned a light golden brown, her hair tousled just enough for him to want to touch it. She licked her fingers. They were sitting at their usual table facing the sea in their favourite restaurant in Portimão. The restaurant was acclaimed as a new experience in food. Normally it was but now Ed was beginning to experience stomach cramps. James was making him lose his appetite fast. For the first time since he arrived, the sun wasn't shining and there was a chill in the air.

'Okay, okay James, don't get your knickers in a twist but I still need to sort things out here.' Ed used his best English public school voice.

'Ed, you don't get it. Your time is up. You come back to the office on Monday – and you stay here – or you're on the streets, man.' James imitated Ed's usual accent.

The phone disconnected. The bastard.

'What is it, Ed?' Charlotte asked. 'Eat. The prawns are yum.'

'They've asked me to go back for a meeting on Monday.'

'Oh no! It's my day off. I thought we were going to Spain. Are you going to go?'

'I don't know, babe.' Ed was thinking fast. In American. They couldn't fire him: he was one of the three directors – unless they were putting a clause in their contracts about each of them having to spend an equal amount of time in the office. Thinking about it, maybe there already was. He was aware he had been spending a lot of money, but it was all in the company's and clients' interest. He'd had to buy the Land Rover to get around those mountain tracks, he'd rented an apartment in Portimão to save on the hotel bills – okay, it was a very nice apartment with a sea view but it wasn't exactly a penthouse. Hell, he'd only been spending about five grand a month. Quite normal in London.

He didn't want Charlotte to know they wanted him to stay in London. She still had another six months on her contract and she was happy here. She had left a rich footballer for him. Their divorce still hadn't come through but Rodrigo had agreed to buy her out of their house in Chelsea and Ed had promised her they would buy a house in Richmond. He had also promised her a yellow convertible Mercedes. And he had promised not to leave her – even for a day.

'Ed! Eat! What's wrong with you?' Charlotte squinted her blue electric eyes into two horizontal beams, magnetising him. He was drawn to her lips and kissed her. Then he dipped a prawn in the garlic sauce and crunched its body, leaving the head between his fingers.

'Nothing, babe.'

His mobile rang again. This time it was Collette giving him the flight details on Monday morning. He told Collette that was right and thanked her, then switched the phone off.

'What was that?' Charlotte asked.

'Just Collette confirming some dates.'

'I thought you were the boss? How can they order you back?'

'Partner.'

'Well, how about we drive up to the mountain and find some more properties? I don't have a rehearsal this afternoon. Maybe if we find some really cheap ones, the other partners will stop giving you a hard time.'

Ed didn't think it would be enough to get out of going back on Monday but it might give him some negotiating power to get the next flight back to Faro. As it happened there were a few properties he would like to have a look at.

'You are a very smart woman, babe. Thank you. That is exactly what we'll do.'

Mustard was parked in the marina. He'd had the foresight to put on the top last night as rain had been forecast. A cold wind blew off the sea.

'Sweet, it's going to rain,' Charlotte said, putting on her cream North Face jacket, looking up at the darkening sky. 'First time in months! At least, Mustard will get a wash. We'll have to change the name to Custard.' She laughed as if she had told the funniest joke ever.

Ed laughed with her.

The first spots came as they drove past Lidl and the Centro Commercial. By the time they reached Maxmat and the roundabout, the rain began to thunder onto the soft roof as if being pelted by rocks.

'Ah, it's coming in through the windows!' Charlotte said.

'Hell, this isn't rain. This is a tsunami!' Ed said. The wipers were going as quick as they could but they could only clear the screen for less than a second.

'Maybe we should wait for it to pass,' Charlotte said.

'No, Mustard will cope. It is an SUV for Christ's sake.'

They turned up the mountain in the direction of Alcalar and Senhora de Verde and slid up the mountain like a salmon upstream. Mustard was getting soggy on the inside as the water seeped in through the stitches. This was not a day to be looking at properties, Ed thought.

'Let's stop for a coffee,' Ed said, pulling into a small café on the left. He switched off the engine and they sat for a minute until they could see nothing but grey streams running down the windscreen. 'Are you ready?'

In the two seconds it took to run from the car to the café, they may as well have jumped into a river. A large puddle formed around them as they arrived at the open door of the dark café. It was a typical Algarvean place, run by a man, about half Ed's size, with a dark moustache, and sold coffee, beer, cheese and ham stale rolls, Snickers and ice-creams. Three men sitting drinking mini bottles of Sagres stared at Charlotte as if she'd landed from Venus. Ed ordered coffees and steered her to the other side of the bar, as far away from the drooling men as possible. He smiled as he read their faces, whatever 'lucky bastard' was in Portuguese. They could drool as much as they wanted.

'I've never seen such rain,' Charlotte said, shaking off her jacket. 'I hope Vicky and Pedro didn't go out in the boat this morning.'

'I shouldn't think so – Pedro would know better.'

'It's actually very beautiful. I never thought I'd say this but after almost six months of sun, it's nice to see rain.'

'*Quanto tempo chove?*' Ed turned round to the mustachioed man with dark green eyes. Envy, Ed thought.

'*Uma semana,*' the man said, waving his hand about and then conferring to the other three men. A week seemed to be the agreed amount of time, maybe a month.

'Sweet!'

They watched the road outside turn into a river and the car-parking area into a lake.

'*Feria*s?' the man asked him.

'*Negócio,*' Ed replied. '*Casas.*'

'*Comprar?*' the man asked, his moustache twitching.

'*Sim.*' This was about the longest conversation he'd had in Portuguese and Charlotte was looking at him in admiration. Ed felt good but he couldn't understand a word of the cascade that followed – especially when the other three joined in and more beers and shots of a white spirit out of an unmarked bottle were ordered. A couple of small glasses found their way over to their table together with the name of a village – Boa Vista – one of the millions. There were three houses apparently for sale. The man then attempted to explain where it was by drawing a map on the napkin.

'*Quanto custa?*' Ed asked.

The man hummed and hawed and then wrote down 100,000. Ed knew this was too much but it may be worth going to see.

'*Quantos donos?*' he asked, wanting to know how many people were involved in the sale.

The man hummed and hawed again and waved his hand dismissively, which Ed didn't think a good sign.

The five houses he had already found were a nightmare as there were about nine hundred owners involved. After three months of negotiating they still didn't seem to be any nearer exchanging contracts. His solicitor had warned him it could take a year to complete the purchase – and that would be good. Ed was able, at least, to have an architect draw up plans in the meantime. Unless it were a new villa, Ed had discovered that buying and selling houses in Portugal was a feudal exercise – many seemed to have been sold for a spring or in exchange for more land, half the owners had died or disappeared, no one knew who the hell owned what. The

Portuguese government just didn't seem to have got to grips with modernizing the system to bring it in line with the rest of Europe. It was crazy. But, when renovated, they would each make several hundred thousand euros in profit. And it was all money that clients wanted to disappear so they were on a win-win situation. A feudal real estate system was balanced by a discrete banking system. And James was moaning about his expenses. Tight-arsed shit.

'It's stopped raining!' Charlotte said.

Everyone peered outside to make sure, in fact, it had stopped. It had.

'Okay, shall we go?' Ed asked and knocked back the white spirit. It burned a hole from his throat down to his stomach.

Charlotte had already drunk hers. He went to get his map out of the car. It was only slightly soggy as he opened it on a table in the café. He tried to get the man to show him where it was, but neither of them could find a Boa Vista and the roads on the map seemed to confuse everyone.

'Bad idea. I have yet to find one map that even vaguely corresponds to the roads,' Ed said.

'Come on, let's go. We'll find it.' Charlotte picked up the napkin.

Ed paid less than a euro for the coffees and they set off again. The roads were still rivers and the air heavy with precipitation, but now light grey clouds raced over the dark sky. Ed felt quite cheerful as they set off. If he could clinch another deal, then he was now sure he would be able to cut short his trip to London.

They climbed into the mountains, up to Casais and turned left and then hit dense grey wool fog. They turned right and wound around the west side of the mountain where the fog suddenly disappeared and an eerie grey light shone onto the mountains. Straggly clouds drifted through the valleys like ghosts.

'Do you know where we are?' he asked Charlotte.

'No.'

'Is this road on the map?'

'No. Shall we stop and ask someone?'

'If we can find someone, babe.'

They turned right at the next junction and then stopped near a parked car. A cluster of houses cut into the mountain slope so that only their ragged terracotta roofs could be seen from the road. Ed pulled over. A tall man was getting in a Mercedes.

'Hey, you speak English?' Ed called out.

'Yes,' the man replied, coming over.

'Do you know of a Boa Vista near here?'

'Several. Including here.' The man laughed. 'Any idea which one?'

'There's supposed to be three houses for sale?'

'Hm, I don't think it's here. There's some for sale down in the valley but that's not Boa Vista. If you go down the path to the house, there's a young girl called Sonia there. She grew up here and more likely to know.'

'Cheers,' Ed said. 'Do you want to wait here?' he asked Charlotte, but she was already getting out.

They went down the track towards a small stone house. Smoke dribbled out of the chimney. Ed knocked on the door and was greeted by shouts of 'it's open'. He pushed the heavy door and found a large room full of people, children, dogs and a cloud of marijuana smoke. Hippies. There were at least three men, two women, five children and three dogs, and possibly more lurking under a table.

'Come in, come in, whoever you are,' an old woman with white hair shouted from a sofa. 'And who is this beautiful lady?'

'Hi there, I'm Ed, and this is Charlotte, and we're looking for a Boa Vista where there are three houses for sale. Do you know where that could be?' The house was clean and relatively tidy but Ed felt claustrophobic. They were all staring at him.

'Are you American or English?' the woman asked.

'Well, I was born in one but lived in the other,' Ed said, wondering what the hell difference it made.

'He's a Brit,' Charlotte said. 'You can tell by the way he turns up his nose.' She laughed. The others joined in.

'I do not,' Ed said indignantly. But he had to give it to her: everyone was now smiling at them.

'But you lived on the West coast. Am I right?'

'About ten years,' said Ed, mildly surprised. 'San Francisco.'

'I thought so. Worked there myself once upon a time.'

'Oh really,' Ed said. Probably in Oakland where all the hippies were.

'Yeah, in the Mission. In the good old days when we were free to smoke. Anyway, this is Boa Vista but, as far as I know, we're not for sale. But they don't tell me everything.' The woman chuckled.

More like a cackle, Ed thought, but he had to admit she was very perceptive. Probably a witch.

150

'Shut up, Mum. You need to talk to Sheila,' a woman, about thirty with long blonde hair, said, stirring some concoction on the stove. 'She's our local estate agent.'

'In Monchique? What agency?'

'She doesn't work for an agency as such. All the Portuguese who want to sell their houses go to her because she speaks Portuguese and knows a lot of foreigners. She lives about four kilometres down the next track on the left.'

'A guy we met on the road said to speak to Sonia?' Ed said.

'Is Sonia here?' the blonde woman asked the other inhabitants.

'She's in the tree house,' a man with a beret said, picking up an axe and getting up from the table. He went to the door and shouted, 'SONIA.'

'So have you been living here long?' Ed asked, once the man with the axe had gone

'Two years.'

'And how do you like it?'

'You know, Ed, there aren't many places left in the world where you can escape the rat-race and be yourself, but this is one of them. Away from the rest of the world. And in the sun. Well, today isn't so good but we need the rain. We don't want any more fires.'

Ed wanted to ask how they lived away from the rat-race as they clearly didn't work but, just then, a young, very attractive Portuguese girl came in.

'Ah, this is Sonia, our young lawyer.'

Sonia blushed.

'Hi there, Sonia,' Ed said. 'Someone said you may know where there's a Boa Vista with three houses for sale?'

Sonia put two fingers to her mouth as she thought.

'Would you like a cup of tea?' the blonde woman asked Charlotte.

'No no, thank you.'

'Yes, I think I know. Go right here for about five kilometres and then turn left. It is a track on the corner – I don't think it is macadam.'

'That's okay, we have a jeep.'

'Okay, then you go straight. I can't remember how long but turn to the south side and you find some ruins.'

'It's on the south side?' Ed said, his heart leaping. He might be saved yet.

'Yes, if that is the Boa Vista you mean.'

'Thank you,' Ed said, pulling his car-keys out of his pocket. He couldn't wait to get out. 'We'll try to find it.'

'Cheers,' Charlotte said.

'By the way, do you know an English guy called Robert?' Ed asked, remembering he had lived in the mountains.

'Robert and Rebecca?' the witch answered. 'A young couple, yes, they live about seven kilometres away.'

'Is he okay?'

'I think so. We don't see much of them. Occasionally, Robert comes here and gets plastered but, otherwise, they stay in.'

'We met him one night in Portimão when he was steaming. He seemed like a nice guy but then he got abusive.'

'He tried to hurt my friend,' Charlotte added.

'Yes, addicts are charming people, but they can not help themselves.'

'Well, we'd better be going. Thanks again for your help.'

'Call in any time.'

Ed put his arm around Charlotte and guided her out the door and up the path in the mist that now clung to the mountains. She held onto his arm, laughing.

'What was that?!' she said.

'A bloody hippy commune,' he said, once they were far enough away not to be heard. The witch might cast a spell.

'Ah, they were very kind.'

Ed grunted as he opened the door for Charlotte and then went round to the driver's side. He didn't trust hippies.

'The good news is that if these houses are on the south side of the mountain they could be worth a fortune.'

He drove back the way they came and found the left turning in the grey mist. It was steep but Mustard climbed up without difficulty and they wound their way further up and around the mountain on a dirt track.

'No road,' Charlotte said. 'I don't think your clients would like that.'

'Roads can be made. Look at those ruins. I think this is it.'

'Look at the stone terraces. It looks beautiful.'

They got out the jeep and wandered around. There were, indeed, three ruins, made of stone, two south facing and one to the west. The roofs had gone but the walls were still intact. Ed marched through the brambles excitedly. These were the best ruins he had seen so far.

As he stood there, the south west wind blew away the clouds just for a second and he could see both Portimão below him and the west coast.

'This is cool,' Charlotte said.

'It certainly is.'

'Can we have a house here?'

'Of course, babe, we can have whatever we want.'

They went back down to the café to talk to the mustachioed man again, who finally introduced himself as Manuel. Ed offered him a seventy thousand euros cash and quick sale. Manuel looked uncertain, twitched his moustache, shook his head and said again one hundred thousand. Charlotte smiled sweetly. Ed went up to eighty and Manuel said that he would think about it. They exchanged mobile numbers and Ed told him his solicitor would be in touch.

'Fish and chips?' he asked Charlotte as they climbed back into Mustard. He was feeling hungry after all that negotiating and he knew fish and chips were her favourite.

'Yum,' she said. 'I haven't got long though.'

He drove to Portimão deep in thought. Even if the sale did go through he knew the office was going to want him back. If they fired him, he would have to go to London anyway. It was the only place he would make money.

'How do you feel about living in the UK again?' he asked Charlotte as they turned off the Alvor roundabout.

'One day, yes. I miss my family.'

Ed smiled to himself. He felt pretty sure she would come with him.

The chip shop was closed down so they went to get a pizza at an Italian restaurant nearby.

'You know what?' Charlotte said, tearing the blunt rolling knife through her pepperoni and pineapple pizza.

'What?' Ed smiled: she had strange tastes. Must be a Market Harborough thing.

'I don't feel like doing the show tonight.'

Ed didn't say anything for a few seconds. This was the first time she had said that. She was usually so keen to get to the casino, but night after night of doing the same show must be tiring.

'Well, don't go then,' he said. 'You don't have to. You've been doing it for six months. You know I'll look after you.'

She smiled. 'Of course I have to. I have a contract and my friends are waiting for me.'

After he'd dropped her off at the casino he called James and told him about the deal. James wasn't impressed and said that they would talk more on Monday. Ed tried again to wiggle out of it but James was adamant he be there at 2 p.m. Monday and stay there. He was already scheduled to see some tricky clients in Prague the following week.

'I have to go back to work in London on Monday,' he told Charlotte after work. They were sitting in their favourite bar in the marina.

'For the meeting? They weren't happy about the houses we found?'

'I think so but I still need to go to this meeting and they have more work for me.'

'So when will you be back?'

'Maybe at the weekend,' he said tentatively. Maybe he could fly from Faro to Prague. 'But I will need to go back again. They're threatening to fire me if I don't and, Charlotte, we need the money.'

'Shit.' She sounded shocked. 'But where does that leave us? You promised not to leave me. I have another six months.' A cloud passed over her face, darkening her blue eyes.

'Will you come with me?'

'No, Ed. I'm not ready to leave my job and friends.' She paused. 'You promised.'

'I'll sort something out,' Ed said. 'Don't worry.'

They drank their *caipirinha* in a heavy silence while the rain thundered down outside.

On Monday morning, Ed, dressed in a grey suit, drove to the airport in the rain. Charlotte was furious with him for leaving and refused to speak to him that morning. He had promised he would come back at the weekend and every weekend. How the hell he was going to pay for the weekly flights and the apartment, he had no idea. But he would find a way. Charlotte deserved the best and he was determined to give her everything he could.

The motorway flashed warnings about the risk of accidents in the rain. He didn't pay them much attention; Mustard had good traction and didn't much like going above 120 km an hour anyway.

And the roads were quiet as always. He could hardly bear to think about London traffic. Hell, the thought of talking bollocks in meetings about investment opportunities, stocks and shares, company criteria, futures and options made his stomach yawn. But he was good at it. That's why he had the job. He could convince a fish to buy a wetsuit, his mother used to say when he worked a Saturday job at Burtons as a teenager. Then, after doing a degree in English Lit and an MBA, he found he could easily convince someone to part with millions of dollars in a company that only existed in name. It was all about confidence. The whole world, the whole capitalist economy, was built on confidence. Who gave a definitive value to things that could only have a subjective value? People like him. Half the time, the money didn't exist but the belief that it did was what kept the financial markets together.

He turned off the motorway as the Faro airport sign appeared sooner than he expected. It seemed a long time since he had arrived in the Algarve. He remembered giving a lift to the two English girls to Luz, Zoe and some young left-wing idealist, school teachers working their asses off for a few grand a year. Madness, but someone had to do the job. Zoe had seen the light in Luz and had called him last month to say that she was back and about to start work at the International School. He remembered liking Zoe, but he hadn't been able to talk much as Charlotte had been there. He didn't want to give Charlotte any reason to be suspicious so he hadn't kept in touch, but he was pleased Zoe had followed her dream. Life was too short not to.

Ed approached some traffic lights and looked at the garages and restaurants. '*Frango piri-piri, Churrasqueira, Pneus, Super Bock, Delta Café.* On a bridge crossing the road was scribbled in red, *Fora Capitalistas!* He remembered seeing the same words on the other side of the road and Zoe asking what 'Fora' meant. Now he knew it meant 'out' or 'away'. *Capitalists Out!* Too late, he thought. The letters were faded. Such ideology belonged to the past, a pre-April 25, 1974 Portugal.

He parked Mustard in the short-term car-park and rolled his suitcase behind him and carried his briefcase. He was early. He would check-in and get a coffee.

He picked up a paper and flicked through it as he sat down with a *bica*. The missing girl story was headlines again. The parents, now suspects, were in England – wise idea. How the hell could they have become suspects? That just didn't make sense. Imagine

155

killing your child and then launching one of the biggest media campaigns in history to find the killer! How dumb would you need to be? On the other hand, how clever. But no, that was ridiculous.

His eyes flicked over other Algarve news and were drawn to a photograph of a familiar face. He scanned the name below. Robert Leicester. His heart skipped. It was him. The same Robert he had met in Portimão and had gone to the casino with. The same Robert he had asked about at that hippy house. Next to the photograph was the big black print: **Young Brit killed in car-crash on 125**. Ed stared at the words. Shit. He couldn't handle his drink but he was a good guy. He scanned the column. It didn't say anything about drink. A truck had overtaken straight into him. Visibility had been bad, the roads slippery. His car had flipped three times and ended up in a field. Hell. Poor Robert. Poor girlfriend.

Ed sat there, holding the page open for what felt like hours. He felt a deep sadness that seemed unwarranted as he had hardly known him. Perhaps it was because, at some deeper level, they were all connected. Individual consciousness separated people but at certain moments, when united by a tragedy, the barriers of consciousness lift and people reacted as one. Empathy, he supposed it was. That's why the whole of America had been united by 9/11 and why Europe and beyond had rallied around the missing girl. In that moment, everyone knows that it could have been any one of them in that building, or their child kidnapped from an apartment, or in a car that crashed. Poor Robert. Ed remembered reading a Zen Buddhist saying about life being as ephemeral as a dewdrop on a lotus leaf. It was true. We are here. And then we are not. He decided there and then that he would go to the stupid meeting but he would come back the next day. Life was indeed too short.

Ed folded the paper and left it on the table. He queued up to go through customs and had to surrender some aftershave he had in his briefcase. He didn't mind. It was better than being a dewdrop on a lotus leaf on a hot day. He shopped for some port to shut up his colleagues and then sat down by the departure gate. He sent Charlotte a message: *At airport. Miss u. Did u c News about Robert?*

He waited ten minutes but she didn't reply. She was probably sleeping. He was queuing up to get through the doors into the pouring rain and onto the bus when his phone finally beeped.

Book me flight 4 2moro. I want 2 b with u.

156

Ed stared at the text in amazement. Then he found his fist punching the air as he forgot about Robert and the ephemerality of life, and wallowed in the joy that those few letters had given him. That's why he loved Charlotte. She was uncomplicated, she followed her heart, and she wasn't afraid to move on. He got on the bus to the plane a happy man. He could sell wetsuits to fish. He would make loads of money and he would build the most spectacular villa for her. He would call it Casa Fora. Away from the world.

A glossary of Portuguese words and expressions

(Most words are given in the singular - plurals are usually made by adding an 's.' Portuguese nouns are prefixed by a definitive article ('a' or 'o') such as 'o bolo', the cake.)

agua – water
avenida – avenue (main street)
azar – bad luck
bacalhau à brás – salted cod dish cooked with chips, egg and onions
baile – a dance, village party
bica – small coffee/espresso
bifana – pork sandwich
bife – slang (derogatory) for English person
boa tarde – good afternoon
bolo – cake
bom dia – good morning
bonita – beautiful
cabrão – slang meaning 'bastard'
calçada – traditional small flat cobblestones used for paving
caldo verde – soup made of cabbage, potatoes, olive oil, salt and slices of *chouriço*
Câmara – the Council
caipirinha – Brazilian alcoholic drink made from *cachaça* (derived from sugar cane) limes and crushed ice
camarão – prawns
caraças – an interjection expressing irony, admiration or impatience
Cartão Utente – national health card
casa – house/home
Centro de Saúde – Health Centre
chouriço – smoked pork sausage (speciality of Monchique)
churrasqueira – grillroom
ciao – bye
comprar – to buy
Correio da Manhã – Morning Post (name of daily newspaper)
'Dança Comigo' – the Portuguese version of 'Come Dancing'
Dona – a female honorary prefix/Mrs or female owner
enxada – type of traditional spade with an angled square
espectacular – spectacular/amazing
Fala Português? – Do you speak Portuguese?
Farmácia – Pharmacy/Chemist
feijoada – bean stew with various types of meat

fogo – literally 'fire' but used here as an interjection of irritation like 'Hell!'

Fora Capitalistas! – Capitalists Out!

filha/filho – daughter/son

Finanças – Finance Office

frango piri-piri – spicy chicken

galão – milky coffee

golo – goal

'Ilha dos Amores' – a soap opera (literally, 'Island of Loves')

imperial – small beer

IVA – VAT

jantar – dinner

lixo – rubbish

lulas – squid

Macieira – a Portuguese brandy

mãe – mother

mais ou menos – more or less

medronho – a white spirit made from the berries of wild strawberry trees, indigenous to Monchique

menina – girl/young woman

'Morangos com Açúcar' – 'Strawberries with Sugar' (a TV series about teenagers)

negócio – business

Obrigada/obrigado – thank you (woman/man)

olá – hi, hello

'O Preco Certo' – 'The Price is Right' (a popular TV game show)

O que é que deseja? – What do you want?

parvos – idiots

pastelaria – typical Portuguese cafe

pastel de nata – custard cream cake

percebes – barnacles

pescador – fisherman

PIDE – the secret police under Salazar

piri-piri – type of red chilli, spicy

pneus – tyres

presunto – ham

Quanto tempo chove? – How long (will) it rain?

Quanto custa? – How much?

Quantos donos? – How many owners?

querido – dear

robalo – sea bass

sabor galinha – chicken flavour

sargo – sea bream

senhor – Mr/Sir/gentlemen (usually prefixed by 'o')
senhora – Mrs/Madam/lady (usually prefixed by 'a')
sereia – mermaid
sim – yes
Só batatas fritas – only chips (French fries)
sonho – literally 'dream' but here a type of donut.
tasca – a traditional Portuguese bar, a small pub
tio – uncle (sometimes shortened to 'Ti'), *tia* – aunt
Três cervejas por favor – Three beers please
trespasse – commercial lease
tudo bem – okay (literally, 'all good')
uma semana – a week
vida – life
vinho verde – a light, slightly fizzy, white wine (literally 'green wine')

ACKNOWLEDGEMENTS

A special thanks to Janice Russell for her invaluable support and editorial advice. Thanks also to Willy Russell for encouragement, and to Wendy and Sandy Buchanan, Paul Tiefenbach, Shelagh Ferreira, Sebastian Castagna, Susana Parker, Odran Jennings, Karin Seidel and Pamela Francis for suggestions and help with both text and images.

This is a work of fiction but, as with any work of fiction, many real life events, anecdotes and people have inspired it. These are many but particular thanks to Tony Lloyd, Phil Hine, Mario Brandão, Lars and Gemma Steffensen, my neighbours, Dona Maria and her family, and everyone at Casa Pedra.